A WEAVER
CHRISTMAS GIFT

BY
ALLISON LEIGH

MILLS
BOON

Published in Great Britain 2014
by Mills & Boon, an imprint of Harlequin (UK) Limited,
Eton House, 18-24 Paradise Road, Richmond, Surrey, TW9 1SR

© 2014 Allison Lee Johnson

ISBN: 978-0-263-91336-1

23-1114

Harlequin (UK) Limited's policy is to use papers that are natural, renewable and recyclable products and made from wood grown in sustainable forests. The logging and manufacturing processes conform to the legal environmental regulations of the country of origin.

Printed and bound in Spain
by CPI. Barcelona

His back was still toward her.

He had a small scar over his right shoulder blade. She'd kissed her way over it dozens of times but had never asked what had caused it.

Why hadn't she asked?

Because she wasn't interested?

Or because she was afraid he wouldn't have told her?

She slowly propped the broom handle against the wall and walked over to him. Her hand wasn't entirely steady when she placed it on his shoulder, but it was a lot steadier than her insides felt.

He stiffened at her touch and looked at her.

She didn't know what was tormenting him.

And maybe comfort wasn't their thing.

But she did know what was.

She leaned forward and slowly pressed her lips against his. She felt him inhale slightly. Resistance, almost.

But not quite.

***

Return to the Double C:
Under the big blue Wyoming sky,
this family discovers true love

There is a saying that you can never be too rich or too thin. **Allison Leigh** doesn't believe that, but she does believe that you can *never* have enough books! When her stories find a way into the hearts—and bookshelves—of others, Allison says she feels she's done something right. Making her home in Arizona with her husband, she enjoys hearing from her readers at Allison@allisonleigh.com or PO Box 40772, Mesa, AZ 85274-0772, USA.

In loving memory of Saing.

Chapter One

"I've decided to get pregnant." As far as sweet nothings went, Jane Cohen's statement didn't rank very high on the scale.

Casey Nathaniel Clay *had* to have heard her wrong. Maybe his head was still reeling from the truly phenomenal sex. Outside of the bedroom, he and Janie couldn't seem to agree on the time of day. Inside the bedroom, though, they were like two halves of a whole.

But in the year since their relationship—for lack of a better word—had moved into the bedroom, not once had either one of them expressed an inclination to take things into the "serious" realm.

He levered himself up on his elbow and peered down at her.

Her long golden hair was tangled around her head, strands clinging to her cheeks and neck, sliding in loose curls down her chest, over her breasts that were still rising and falling as she caught her breath from not one but—hell, yeah, if he didn't mind counting 'em—two orgasms.

He dragged his stupidly reluctant gaze upward to meet her coffee-colored eyes. "What's that you say?"

She pressed her lips together. They were the same soft pink as her nipples. "Don't pretend you didn't hear me." Annoyance rang in her voice as she impatiently pushed her hair from her face. "I was perfectly clear."

Ordinarily, people tended to consider Casey a relatively intelligent guy. His degrees from MIT supported that opinion. But just then, he didn't seem capable of forming much of a coherent thought, much less a reasonable response.

What the hell are you talking about? was in the forefront of his mind. And he was pretty sure that wasn't what Janie was looking for.

She seemed to know what he was thinking anyway, because her lips tightened even more.

Looking disgusted, she rolled her eyes and shoved his shoulders aside, disentangling her warm legs from his, and slid off the bed. "Cool the panic jets, Casey." Her voice was tart as a bowl of lemon juice with the closest supply of sugar a few counties away. "I wasn't suggesting I wanted to get pregnant by *you*."

The words stung more than she'd ever know.

He eyed her, wondering why he'd thought that getting into bed with the infernal woman was a good idea in the first place. But that was just what happened when a man followed his baser nature. "Then why on earth did you bring it up now?" he groused.

She made that impatient sound that only women seemed to know how to make, the sound meant to convey he was missing something completely obvious to anyone with a half a brain. The sound that pretty much meant he was dumber than a box of rocks. She retrieved her robe from the back of the bedroom door and slid into it, yanking the belt around her narrow waist.

The action only served to draw attention to her breasts.

They were perfect, those breasts. Surprisingly full for someone with such a lean, athletic figure. Her legs were perfect, too. And don't get him started on her butt—

"Because if I want to have a baby, all this has to change." Her tone—superior and vaguely snooty—pulled his attention back to her face. She was waving her hand toward the bed. Toward him.

The pink robe was thin. It clung lovingly to her curves as she moved around the room, snatching up their strewn articles of clothing.

Again, he focused with an effort and bunched the blanket around his hips as he sat up. This particular turn of the conversation made sprawling there naked as a jaybird seem ill-advised. "Change," he repeated warily.

She made that sound again and tossed him his jeans. She hadn't found his boxers yet, but he didn't care. He got off the bed and pulled on the jeans anyway. "Obviously, I can't proceed with my plan while we're—" she waved her hand again "—whatever we are."

"Friends with benefits," he hazarded. It was a safer definition than some he could have offered.

She snorted softly. "I think *friends* is overstating."

He grimaced, not liking the fact that her words bit any more than he liked the way the night had taken such an abrupt turn south. "We're friends," he grumbled. Maybe it was an exaggeration, but he was pretty sure it wasn't an outright lie.

Her eyebrows rose as if she didn't believe the claim any more than he did. She'd pulled on the pair of black horn-rimmed glasses that she rarely wore when she was working at Colbys, the bar and grill she'd bought five years ago. The lenses made her eyes look unnaturally large.

The first time he'd seen her wearing them, he'd decided the bookish glasses made her look even sexier.

Oddly approachable.

Times like this, he wished he'd never seen her in them, considering they'd ended up in bed together almost immediately after.

"Please," she drawled. "In what way are we friends? There's nothing on which we *ever* agree."

Even over that point, he had to differ. "You pour a decent beer. And you came to your senses finally and stopped charging to use the pool tables."

"High praise. We don't have a friendship. We have a…a sexship." She didn't look at him as she tossed him his T-shirt. It still hit him square in the chest. "I want to have a baby," she said again. "But I have no desire to be a single mother." She bent over again and the lapels of her robe gaped, giving him an eyeful of creamy skin. "Call me old-fashioned, but I intend to be married first." She straightened and dropped his socks on the corner of the bed in front of him.

Here's your hat; what's your hurry?

"And then stay that way," she added flatly. "My mom never married my dad. After she kicked him out, she struggled every single day raising my sister and me. Trust me. I am *not* doing that. I want a husband."

His head felt oddly light. He sat on the bed and shoved his feet into the socks. "You told me you'd had one of those and couldn't imagine wanting another."

"I don't want another husband like *Gage*," she said, as if Casey was missing the point. "He was a complete workaholic." She gave Casey a pointed look, evidently accusing him of fitting the description, too. "I want some-one who will put *me* first."

"Someone who'll let you run the show, you mean," he muttered. One thing he'd learned about Janie Cohen was that she liked to think she was always in the driver's seat.

She gave him one of her snippy smiles. "At least *I* have a plan."

He scratched his chin. He'd forgotten to shave before coming to see her. He usually tried to remember to, be-cause her fair skin was so easily marred by his whiskers. But he'd had a long day and hadn't thought beyond see-ing her as soon as possible. "Am I supposed to take some hint there that you think I don't?"

"I'm not talking about you."

Maybe he'd spent too many hours studying computer feeds, because following her thought process was giving him a headache. "And the plan is to get a husband so you can get knocked up?"

"I'm a thirty-two-year-old woman," she said. "Knocked up is for teenagers who don't know better."

"Like your mom."

She made a face and ignored that. "Obviously, I'm not getting any younger. So I need to get started." She waved him out of the way and smartly flipped the sheets into some semblance of order.

He had the feeling he was being flipped away just as easily as the wrinkles in the fabric.

"Just like that." He snapped his fingers in her face. "What are you going to do? Order yourself up some hus-band out of *Mail-Order Husbands Weekly*?"

She hesitated as if she was actually giving the idea some thought.

"I was kidding," he said hastily.

"There are mail-order brides," she said. "Guess there

are probably mail-order husbands. But no." She fluffed the pillows, put them back at the head of the bed and turned to face him, her hands propped on her narrow hips. She looked up at him through her glasses with her vaguely buggy brown eyes.

And he was damned if he didn't want to tumble her right back onto that bed and mess up the sheets all over again, even if she was annoying as hell.

"I intend to find a husband right here in Weaver."

He barked out a laugh before he could stop himself.

"You think it's *funny*?" Her voice went silky but her eyes were as chilly as a Weaver winter. "You think I'm incapable of finding a man who might want to put a ring on it?"

"I think the pickings around Weaver are gonna be a tad slim for a woman like you," he answered, trying unsuccessfully to curtail his untimely amusement. Their small Wyoming town wasn't exactly a mecca of single, eligible adults. Despite the consumer electronics company he ostensibly worked for, Cee-Vid, the town was first and foremost a ranching community. Always had been. Always would be. And Jane—for all of her talents—didn't strike him as a typical rancher's wife.

A niggle of guilt pricked his mind over that. Among his own relatives, he could count a passel of ranchers. None of their wives were particularly "typical" either. There were doctors, accountants, business owners...

Jane had propped her hand on her hip and was staring down her nose at him. Considering she was about a foot shorter, it was a feat he might have admired under other circumstances.

"*A woman like me*," she repeated. Her eyebrow arched. "Want to explain that one, Clay?"

"Untie the knots in your little white panties, sport," he

returned. "I just meant you're a tad...classy...for some of the guys around here."

She didn't look particularly soothed. "I run a bar where the dress code just means wiping the manure off your cowboy boots before you come in," she snapped. "How on God's green earth does that make me classy?"

Stubborn. Headstrong. A straight shooter who didn't suffer fools. He kept the descriptors to himself. At one time or another—often all at once—they fit the woman standing in front of him. She was also beautiful as hell, uncommonly unpretentious and a challenge to his senses as well as his brain.

He dragged his T-shirt on over his head and pretended not to notice the way her gaze dropped, just for a second, to run hungrily over his abdomen before he yanked the white cotton over it.

Sex.

That was what the two of them were good at.

Exceedingly good at, they'd discovered. And, he'd thought, to their mutual satisfaction and content.

Now she wanted more. A baby. A husband.

"What about love?" he asked.

If he hadn't been watching closely, he might have missed the way her gaze flickered. "What about it?"

"That's usually the reason people get married, isn't it? What's in this plan of yours when it comes to that?"

It was the first week of September, but Jane still felt a shiver jolt down her spine.

She casually moved away from Casey, crossing the room to retrieve the garish Hawaiian-print shirt he'd been wearing unbuttoned over his T-shirt when he'd arrived. The garment was hideous in the extreme, but it smelled of him and that wasn't hideous at all. No. The scent was warm. Slightly spicy. Definitely heady.

She shivered again and turned to carelessly fling the shirt at him. She wished she could fling away the man's effect on her as easily. "I'm not looking for love," she said blithely. "Just a—"

"Legitimate sperm donor." As he caught the shirt, he seemed to look right into the depths of her with his silvery-gray eyes.

"Why does it even matter to you?" She kept her voice tart as much for self-preservation as from habit. Unless she was mindless with lust in his arms, it was always easier to spar with the tall man with the butterscotch-colored hair than have any sort of serious conversation. Mostly because she was never entirely sure what exactly he was thinking.

Despite his outwardly laid-back style, she'd never made the mistake of thinking Casey Clay actually *was* laid-back. He was too intense for that. And much, much too secretive.

When it came to him, sex was easy.

It was all the rest that was impossible.

"Be glad that I'm under no illusions that *you* might be a candidate," she finished.

His mobile, scrumptious lips twisted wryly. "Janie." He pressed his splayed hand against his chest. "I might be wounded."

"But you're not," she deadpanned, then rolled her eyes when his cell phone chirped and he grabbed it off the nightstand. "Naturally." It wasn't the first time his phone had interrupted them. At least this time it had waited until *after*.

She went into the adjoining bathroom while he answered. Not particularly proud that she tried to listen in but trying anyway, she twisted her tangled hair up into a clip at the back of her head.

However, his voice was low, his words brief, revealing as little as they ever did.

She returned to the bedroom just as he was pocketing the phone. "Let me guess." She might not have overheard the reason he was being called away, but she had a good idea where he was going and she smiled facetiously. "Somebody's computer is on the fritz at Cee-Vid and you have to go save the day. Or the night, as it were."

His gaze slid over her, setting off another darned shiver. "That's why I get the big bucks."

Cee-Vid produced video games. He was in charge of the computer systems there, but she couldn't imagine what could be so critical at the business that he'd get called at all hours of the night in the way he often was even if he'd already been there all day.

She'd have suspected him of having a wife if Weaver weren't so small that such a fact would have been impossible to hide.

Everyone knew everyone else's business around town. Or so it had seemed to her since she'd moved there five years ago. As a result, it was still an amazing thing to her that they'd been able to keep their…encounters…private.

He stepped up to her and raised his hand. She stiffened. Not from fear, but because he was drawing a single fingertip slowly down her cheek and she felt a corresponding line of heat work down her spine. He was a truly impossible man, but for some unfathomable reason, he charged her batteries in a way nobody else had ever done.

And the faint half smile on his face warned her that he knew exactly the reaction he elicited.

Dammit.

"Mebbe you figure you don't need to order up a dose of *love* with this prospective husband of yours, but you didn't say anything about chemistry either." He waited a knowing beat. "Don't pretend you don't want passion. I know otherwise."

She wanted to move back from him in the worst way, but she knew that was what he was expecting, so she held her ground. "Passion is overrated," she said.

His eyes took on an unholy glint. "It gets a couple into the bedroom, sport. I've always heard that making babies is a lot more fun when it's done the old-fashioned way. Or were you thinking you'd be able to get yourself in the family way while keeping your convenient husband at arm's length?"

"Medical science is a wonderful thing." She savored the satisfaction of actually igniting some surprise in his silvery gaze. "But no. I want a husband. I want to make a baby—or babies—with him." Though she hadn't expected it, over the past several months she'd come to realize she wanted the same thing her little sister had. She wanted to be more than a business owner. She wanted a real home. A real family. "I expect to get pregnant in the usual manner."

His lips twisted again. He was probably thinking she was nuts. She knew he wasn't jealous. He didn't care about her that way. He cared that she gave as good as she got when their clothes started hitting the floor.

Chemistry. She and Casey Clay had it in spades.

But that was all they had.

There was no future. He'd made that abundantly clear from the very start. She might have had a change of mind along the way, but she wasn't foolish enough to believe that he had.

Or that he ever would.

"Borrow your sister's baby for a week," he advised. "The allure might wear off after 24/7 of diapers and bottles and crying." He tugged the garish shirt over his wide shoulders. "Hell. Get a puppy. Angeline's gonna have a whole new litter of 'em in a month or so that'll be needing homes. I'll hook you up with one."

She just eyed him. Angeline, she knew, was his sister who lived with her husband and family over in Sheridan. They'd met once in passing some time ago. In passing because family get-togethers weren't part of Casey and Jane's deal. He didn't invite her to any—even though, with the Clay family, who had fingers in nearly every pie in town, there seemed to be many.

And if he had invited her, she'd have told him he was out of his tree anyway. They weren't dating. They were just sleeping together. Nothing more.

"This isn't like deciding I want a new pair of shoes. Or a new dog. I've never even had a dog."

He gave her a vaguely shocked look and she wished she'd kept that tidbit to herself.

"I want a husband," she added quickly. "A family of my own. I want it when I wake up and when I go to sleep and I'm too old now not to do something about it!"

Something came and went in his eyes as he put on his worn tennis shoes. He didn't even bother tying the laces. "If you're bound and determined, I could probably set you up with a couple candidates."

She nearly choked. "I don't need your help finding a husband."

He shrugged. "Suit yourself, sport." Then his head swooped and his mouth caught hers in a fast, thorough kiss that left her knees weak and her insides hot. When he lifted his head again, she was certain there was amusement lurking at the corners of his lips. "Just let me know if you change your mind."

About *what*? Ending things with him? Allowing him to set her up with someone else?

"I won't change my mind," she said stiffly. Removing him from the equation would best be accomplished cold turkey. Like a swift yank that removed an adhesive bandage. "So the next time you're looking for a bedmate, you'll have to look elsewhere." The fact that he wouldn't have to look hard wasn't lost on her. Despite his unfathomable dedication to the ugly shirts of the world, Casey Clay was stupefyingly gorgeous. Intelligent and humorous despite his secretive nature. In her very own bar, Jane had witnessed countless women throwing themselves at him.

She had never been one of them. Their relationship, their sexship, hadn't been planned. It had been more like a head-on collision neither one of them had predicted.

"It won't be the same." His lips crooked. "Nobody gives good…bickering…like you."

She pressed her lips together, not wanting to be amused, particularly now, and headed downstairs to the back door. He never parked in front on the street, where his truck might be noticed. She yanked open the door. It was almost midnight and outside, everything was quiet and still. "I'd like to say it's been a pleasure—"

"It's been more than that," he drawled as he stepped past her. "Since passion isn't factored in this plan of yours, you'll probably want to remember what it feels like when you're working your way through your matrimonial prospects. But if you find yourself in need of a reminder, you know where to find me."

"Working at Cee-Vid," she said smoothly. "Because nothing's more important than keeping those video games coming." Then, before she changed her mind, she pushed the door closed behind him.

If she'd wanted confirmation that Casey would never be interested in redefining their friends-with-benefits relationship, she'd certainly gotten it.

She just wished that it didn't hurt quite so much.

Chapter Two

Inside his office at Cee-Vid, Casey entered a code on his computer that revealed a security panel in one wall. Cee-Vid had been producing some of the most popular video games in the world for the past few decades. But behind the front, the company did a heck of a lot more as a location of Hollins-Winword, an equally successful organization that hardly anyone in the world knew existed. International security. Black ops. Hollins-Winword did it all and they did it well. And right now, they had an asset on the ground in Nepal named Bax Kennedy who had missed his last two check-ins. Casey's mind should have been strictly on that fact. But it wasn't.

It was on Jane Cohen.

He stepped up to the security panel that looked like a small wall mirror and stared into the iris scanner.

She wanted to get pregnant. Have a baby.

The scan completed and a numeric panel lit behind the false mirror's surface.

Why hadn't he seen it coming? She was a woman. Past thirty. There were enough females among the Clay clan for him to know perfectly well that her desire for a family wasn't unnatural. Hell, his entire extended family believed in having kids.

It was what the Clays did.

Except for him.

He tapped in another code on the smooth surface and heard the nearly soundless, hollow release that came from somewhere inside the wall. A moment later, part of the wall moved, revealing itself as the door it actually was, and he stepped through into the cavernous communications center they called Control.

"Status?"

Seth Banyon leaned back in his chair and stretched, looking relaxed even though his eyes never stopped roving the bank of screens covering the wall in front of him. "Same."

Casey felt the automatic door closing behind him and he moved across the large blue-lit room to stand behind his associate. Like Casey, Seth collected a paycheck that showed that he worked for Cee-Vid. But also like Casey, his real employer was hidden deep and well beneath that. "This was a simple assignment," he said. "All Bax had to do was escort the emir's niece back to college."

"Without drawing attention to the fact that she wasn't where she was supposed to be in the first place. Money," Banyon muttered. "More trouble than it's worth, if you ask me."

The emir had plenty of it. His affection for his only sister's three children was well-known. When whispers of a possible kidnapping attempt had reached him, he'd reached out to Hollins-Winword to discreetly resolve matters.

Casey had two sisters and from them, four nephews and a niece. They were still children but whatever their ages, he knew there wasn't much he wouldn't do to help keep them safe.

He stepped around Banyon and tapped a few keys on one of the keyboards that surrounded the room. The uppermost screen on the wall in front of them shifted from a satellite image to a photograph of the emir's niece and nephews. "This isn't about money. It's about a power struggle between the emir and his despot of a second cousin. And a whole lot of oil behind them. Where are the other two?"

"Safe behind the walls of their London estate in the loving arms of their mama."

"At least that's something. We've only got Samira to worry about. Wish to hell she would have stayed in London instead of going out on this mission trip of hers."

A series of electronic chimes sounded and a moment later, another interior door slid open and the man in charge stepped inside.

To most of the world—including the regular employees of Cee-Vid, who didn't know anything else was going on beneath the surface—Tristan Clay was merely the brilliant mind behind Cee-Vid.

To a select few, he was close to the top of the food chain inside Hollins-Winword. And to Casey, Tristan Clay was not only his boss but his uncle.

The older man's piercing blue gaze went straight to the bank of screens. "Where're we at?"

Protocols were always followed whenever an asset or an operative went off plan. It was easier for Casey to work through them than it was for him to think about Janie's "plan," and he nudged Banyon out of the seat and took his position at the controls. "Last contact was thirty-six hours ago." His fingers started flying over the console, satellites high above the world snapped to attention, and Casey did the only thing in the world he figured he was meant to do.

He kept Hollins-Winword's own safe.

"You *do* realize that if women could just snap their fingers and find the perfect man, the entire chocolate industry might crumble to dust?" Hayley Templeton's slender fingers hovered indecisively over the opened box of Godiva delectables sitting on top of the gleaming wood bar at Colbys.

Jane wasn't indecisive at all. She plucked a heart-shaped piece from the box and bit it in half, sighing a little over the explosion of bliss on her taste buds. "I know I can't just snap my fingers," she countered. If her digits possessed such magic, she'd have waved them over Casey and he wouldn't have bothered offering up his friends and associates to put their heads in her matrimonial noose.

He would have given his neck to her willingly.

Instead, he'd bolted.

Just as she'd known he would.

The chocolate suddenly lost its appeal, but she ate the second half of the heart anyway before rinsing her hands at the bar sink and pulling the latest rack of glasses fresh from the dishwasher built into the cabinets below the bar. "Other women manage to find spouses here in Weaver. So why can't I?"

Hayley finally selected a chocolate and replaced the lid on the gold box. "Get that away from me before I eat the rest."

"They are *your* chocolates," Jane reminded her. Her friend had brought them with her when she'd stopped by the bar and grill that afternoon.

"And I expect you to save me. I haven't been running with Sam Dawson four times a week only to have a box of chocolates, given to me by a grateful patient, going straight to my hips." Hayley groaned. "Sam's a slave driver. You'd think she'd have a little sympathy for her friends."

Sam Dawson was a deputy with the sheriff's department. "She gave me a parking ticket the other day. Sam doesn't have any sympathy for anyone." Jane took pity on Hayley and tucked away the golden box of temptation before unloading the rack of glasses onto the shelves on the wall behind her. "I think she was just making up for the fact that I kicked her butt in racquetball last week."

"I honestly don't know how I ended up with such competitive friends." Hayley propped her elbows on the bar and glanced around. At three in the afternoon, the place was busy with families having late lunches or early dinners, but the bar itself was quiet.

It would pick up later, though. Friday nights were always packed at Colbys. The establishment had been a Weaver staple since long before Jane had bought it from the family of a friend she'd known since college. Well, she amended mentally, since her ex-husband, Gage Stanton, had staked her purchase of the place.

What was unusual, though, was Hayley stopping in at that hour of the day. Finished with the sparkling clean pilsner glasses, Jane turned back to her friend. "So what's wrong?"

Hayley ran her hand down the sleek tail of her ponytail. "Who says anything's wrong?"

Jane shook her head a little. When it came to the town of Weaver, even after several years there, they were still relative newcomers. As was Sam Dawson. But the three of them had all struck up an enduring friendship. She dumped ice into a glass, filled it with diet cola and set it in front of her friend. "You know bartenders are the best listeners. Comes with the territory."

Hayley pulled a face and reached for the drink. "Counselors are the best listeners," she corrected her. "My PhD in psychology says so." She twisted the glass between her fingers. "Just some family dissension. Evidently, after more than thirty years of estrangement, my grandmother has been trying to mend fences with my dad and my uncle, and they're not having any of it."

Because the bar was so quiet and the restaurant section had its own complement of servers, Jane pulled up the stool she kept behind the bar and sat down to sip at her own soda. "This is their mom you're talking about?"

Hayley nodded. "Vivian Archer Templeton." She drew out the name, then lifted her shoulders. "She lives in Pittsburgh and has been making noises about visiting them in Braden. I think Daddy and Uncle David are wrong and should be more receptive. They didn't really take kindly to my input. As far as they're concerned, she's just a selfish, filthy-rich snob who'll never change."

"And Dr. Templeton *never* goes off duty," Jane murmured. "Is she really rich?"

"Loaded. She married into it, evidently, when she married her first husband. My grandfather. Steel or something." Then Hayley seemed to shake off her thoughts. "Back to you and the great husband hunt. Believe me. I completely understand a ticking biological clock." Her lips twisted ruefully as she patted her chest. "Ticktock, ticktock here, too. None of us are getting any younger. But women these days do have babies without rushing into a marriage."

"Not me." Suddenly restless, Jane grabbed a clean bar towel and moved to the far end to start polishing the long wooden surface. "I know society has changed since my mother did it, but that doesn't mean single parenting is easy. As a family counselor, you would know that more than anyone."

"True enough." Hayley rested her elbow on the bar and propped her chin on her hand. "Though your mom didn't make that choice alone. Your dad walked out on all of you, didn't she?"

"She made him leave." And once he was gone, her mother had pretended he never existed at all. Since her parents had never married, doing so had been horribly easy.

Hayley made a soft *mmming* sound.

Jane pulled out the chocolate box again and waved it under Hayley's nose. "Stop looking at me like I'm one of your patients or I'm going to open this up again."

Hayley pushed the box aside. "Fine. Since we've established the fact that you can't just snap your fingers for a husband, what *do* you plan to do about it?" There was a smile in her eyes as she nodded toward the fishbowl on one end of the counter. "Have a drawing like you do for a free meal?"

"I've heard worse ideas." Jane put away the chocolates again and eyed the bowl where people dropped in a business card or simply a name and phone number, scratched on the back of their receipt, for her weekly drawing. "I wonder if any guys would bother to enter."

Hayley laughed. "For a chance with you? Half the men in this town—married or not—have probably had a fantasy or two about you."

Jane grimaced. "I seriously doubt that." She certainly hoped not. "Kind of an ick factor there, Dr. Templeton."

"I know who isn't at all icky." Her friend smiled slyly. "Casey Clay."

"I should never have told you about him," Jane muttered.

Hayley's smile widened. "If I were your therapist—"

"You're not."

"—I would suggest that you think about your feelings where he's concerned."

"I have no feelings," Jane lied. "The man is impossible. He can't even keep his truck clean. The last time I saw it, he had a pile of junk on the passenger seat that you wouldn't believe."

"Good family." Hayley held up her index finger. "All of the Clays who live in the area are plain old good people." She held up a second finger. "Well over six feet tall. Exceptional shape." Her eyes twinkled. "Thick golden-brown hair and gray eyes. In other words, the usual good genes for that particular family." She held up her third finger. "Intelligent." Her pinky finger joined the others. "Good sense of humor." She added her thumb. "Single, heterosexual male. Messy truck notwithstanding, I could go on."

"Then you date him."

Hayley laughed softly and glanced around the empty bar before leaning forward over her crossed arms. "You're the one who's been secretly sleeping with him for the past year. Seems to me he'd be your best candidate. And you realize if you're not dating him, someone else will. Isn't that going to bother you?"

Jane shrugged as if it wouldn't, even though the very idea of it made her more than a little ill. "What he does isn't my concern. He's allergic to commitment anyway. He'll tell you that himself." He'd certainly said that exact thing to her more than once. Before they'd ended up in bed together, as well as after.

"You used to say the same thing about yourself."

"Some allergies cure themselves, I guess. I want a baby." She also was afraid she wanted Casey, but that was never going to happen. Cutting her losses now would be easier than having to later.

Hayley's expression turned sympathetic. "I know you do, sweetie. But—" she lifted her hand peaceably "—this is just a little food for thought. Sometimes people will focus harder on a secondary issue in order to avoid dealing with a primary issue."

"Casey Clay is not my primary issue," Jane said flatly. "I knew exactly where we stood with each other and that's why I ended things with him last night." It was her own bad luck she'd allowed her emotions to creep in where he was concerned. She dragged the fishbowl over and dumped the half-dozen business cards and receipts out onto the bar top. "I can't be hunting for a husband when I'm sleeping with him."

She tugged off the card taped to the front of the fishbowl that described the weekly free-meal drawing and turned it over to the blank side. She pulled a pen from her pocket and uncapped it. "So what do you think? Win a free meal with Jane Cohen? Entries open to single men only?"

Hayley chuckled wryly and covered her eyes. "Girlfriend, you are just asking for trouble."

"Is she *serious*?"

At the sound of his cousin's voice, Casey looked up from the pool table where he was lining up his next shot. Erik was holding the fishbowl that usually sat on the end of Colbys' wooden bar top.

Casey shrugged and focused on his shot again. "She gives away a free meal every week. Has for a long time. So what?" It was Friday night. Colbys was typically crowded. And even though Casey hadn't really wanted to meet his cousin here after his encounter with Jane the night before, he hadn't been able to come up with a good excuse not to. He'd located Bax, the missing asset in Nepal. He and the emir's niece were no worse for wear, and though Bax hadn't yet gotten her returned to her London apartment, at least they knew she hadn't been abducted by her father's terroristic cousin. For now, things were back on track.

At least in that world.

Casey involuntarily looked over to the bar where Jane was busy pouring out drinks. Her long hair was pulled back in a thick ponytail that swayed every time she turned to grab a glass off the shelves behind her. She was in her usual working garb of black T-shirt, jeans and cowboy boots, but the fact that *she* wore them transformed the ordinary into something extraordinary.

She was a smart cookie. Never missed a thing. So he knew she was well aware of his presence. She just hadn't bothered to give him so much as a glance.

He, on the other hand, couldn't stop looking toward her.

He took his shot and sent the balls rolling.

None landed where he'd intended.

"Not just her usual free meal," Erik was saying. He set the fishbowl on the rail near Casey before leaning over the table with his cue. "Looks to me like she's shaking up the status quo between you two."

Erik was the only one who knew of Casey's involvement with the woman.

Past involvement, he reminded himself, since she'd pretty much kicked him to the curb the evening before.

He dragged his attention away from the smooth curves

of Jane's lightly tanned arms. "She's over twenty-one," he said casually. "Free to do whatever she wants."

"That why your game seems shot to hell all of a sudden?"

He ignored Erik and glanced at the fishbowl.

When the words on the side of it penetrated, he very nearly tore the white index card free of the tape holding it in place.

She certainly wasn't wasting any time with her husband hunt.

He held up the glass bowl, studying the contents. The damned thing was more than half full. Evidently, adding herself to the free-meal menu had spurred a whole new interest in her drawing.

"She's out of her tree," he muttered. Glancing around the bar, he spotted Keith Lambert, who was one of the game designers on the legitimate side of Cee-Vid, whom his uncle had recently hired straight out of school. The young guy, his usual plaid bow tie in place, was sitting in a corner booth with a couple other Cee-Viders. All three of them had their noses stuck in their cell phones as if they didn't know how to communicate face-to-face.

Casey moved over to their table and plunked the fishbowl in the center of it, startling the young men. He knew plenty of designers who didn't look as if they needed a good dose of sunshine, but these guys sure did. Collectively, they were pretty much the embodiment of every clichéd computer-geek joke. "Step right up, guys." He tapped the bowl with Jane's hand-printed invitation stuck to the side.

Keith squinted through his horn-rimmed glasses as he read the card. Then he craned his neck to look at Jane behind the bar across the room. "Sweet. I hear older women are hotter in the sack."

Casey's fingers curled. He'd bet his favorite shirt that Keith had never even kissed a girl, hot or otherwise. The same went for his pallid companions. Jane would make mincemeat of all of them before they ever got to dessert, much less anything after that. "So I've heard," he said blandly. "Might consider stuffing the ballot box to up the odds in your favor."

Keith's Adam's apple bobbed. "Cheat?"

"She doesn't specify one entry," Casey reasoned. "The only restriction is you have to be single." He plucked the pen from Keith's ink-stained shirt pocket and tossed it on the table in front of him. "Go for it, man."

Keith's buddies were grinning and nearly bouncing in their booth.

Before he either rolled his eyes or knocked their heads together, Casey returned to his pool game.

But the game was already done. Erik had already cleared the felt. "You owe me twenty," his cousin said, looking as if he wanted to laugh.

Casey pulled out his wallet and slapped down the money. "Why aren't you home in the loving arms of your wife, anyway? Wedded bliss already wearing off?" His cousin and Isabella had gotten married the previous year and Casey knew good and well that they were besotted with each other.

"Izzy's in Cheyenne with Lucy for a few days. They've taken some of their students for a dance workshop down there before school starts up next week for the fall."

Lucy was another of their cousins, and she ran the only dance school in Weaver. Isabella taught a few classes there. "Little girls in tap shoes or big girls in belly-dancing costumes?" He felt his gaze straying back toward the bar but mastered the impulse and picked up his beer mug instead. "Your wife teaches both."

Erik grinned wryly. "Don't forget the pole-dancing-for-fitness classes." He rubbed his jaw. "She actually had me try it, you know."

Casey nearly dropped his beer. Despite being Tristan Clay's son, Erik had gone into the ranching side of the Clay dynasty. But even in that, he had to go his own way, choosing to maintain his own brand rather than use the Double-C brand started by their grandfather, Squire, that was already one of the most well-known in the state. His cousin was salt-of-the-earth steady and more than a little old-fashioned, so the image that sprang to mind was one for the record books. "Swinging around on a *pole*?"

His cousin looked chagrinned. "It's harder than you think. I fell on my ass. Izzy's never gonna let me live it down."

For the first time since Jane's wanna-baby bombshell, Casey actually laughed. "She's not the only one. I just don't want to picture it in my mind. Afraid it'll do permanent brain damage. What about Murph?"

Murphy had been Isabella's teenage ward when she'd first come to Weaver. Now she was legally his mother and soon Erik would legally be his father. And Casey could rib the other man—who was his best friend as much as his cousin—about anything under the sun, including his new family, but he knew Erik had never been happier.

Erik grinned. "He was no more successful at it than I was, but you didn't hear that from me. So what's Jane really up to?"

Casey hid his frown in his beer and shrugged. He hadn't shared Jane's sudden life goal with Erik, mostly because it might lead to discussions he didn't want to have. "Don't ask me."

Erik gave him a disbelieving look, but thankfully

let the matter drop. Instead, he waved at the pool table. "Double or nothing?"

"Rack 'em up." Casey's gaze started to slide to the bar but he physically turned his back so he was looking toward the front door instead.

He took one last glance toward Keith. He and his buddies were busily stuffing business cards into the fishbowl.

God help them all.

Chapter Three

Jane managed a tight smile before shutting her front door in Prospect Number Three's face.

The past three weeks—especially the past three Thursday-night dates with Number Three and his predecessors, One and Two—had been abysmal.

Number One, a real estate agent from nearby Braden, hadn't understood the difference between Thursday and Friday and, after standing her up at the restaurant where she'd arranged to meet him, had instead accused her of standing *him* up when he'd expected her there the following night. She hoped he handled his real estate transactions with more accuracy.

Number Two was a veterinary technician from right here in Weaver. Nothing really wrong with Two. Except he spent the entire evening talking about his exgirlfriend, with whom he was clearly still in love. Jane had felt like a matronly aunt, advising him to contact the girl and make things up with her.

And Number Three…

Jane heaved a sigh and leaned back against the door she'd just closed. Number Three might possess some genius intellect, but conversing about anything outside of the video games he designed had been impossible. And then the nitwit had believed she was going to invite him in for some dessert of a very personal variety after the dinner she had paid for.

She wouldn't have gone out with him at all, because he worked at Cee-Vid, which was too closely connected to Casey, except that Number Three—like Two and One—had won the weekly fishbowl drawing.

The first thing she was going to do when she went to the bar the next day was throw out the fishbowl and all of its contents. If the only way she could get a date was through a drawing, she'd be better off looking into that whole mail-order-husband thing.

She rubbed at the pain between her eyebrows caused by the past ninety minutes of mind-numbing boredom and headed into her bedroom, shedding her knee-length sweater dress as she went. It was still relatively early, and she was too keyed up to relax. So she changed into jeans and a bright red turtleneck and headed back out to Colbys.

She'd throw out the fishbowl when she got there.

Her assistant manager, Merilee, had worked for Jane long enough not to show her surprise when she walked in the door on what was supposed to be her night off. Jane went straight to the glass bowl and dumped the contents in the trash, along with the card displaying the "rules" of the drawing. Then she stuck the bowl beneath the counter and glanced around the sparsely occupied tables.

She didn't want to acknowledge what she was really doing: looking to see if Casey happened to be around playing pool. The pool tables were his primary interest where Colbys was concerned. Far more than any libations that she offered in the bar or food that they served in the restaurant.

But the tables were quiet.

"Everything all right?" Merilee asked when Jane sighed a little.

"Just fine." Jane grabbed a bottled water, then pushed through the door to the storeroom, where all the shelves were neatly packed with supplies. She went into the minuscule office squeezed between the storage room and the draft cooler where her beer kegs were housed and threw herself down on the squeaky chair behind the beat-up metal desk.

But instead of opening the water bottle or booting up her computer, she picked up the photograph of her sister that sat in a wood frame on the corner of the desk. Julia was cuddling her infant son, Drake, and Julia's husband, Don, was cradling them both in his arms. Happiness radiated from their eyes.

Jane rubbed her thumb over the picture glass, melancholy weighting her down. Julia, who now lived in Montana, was two years younger than Jane. She and Don had been married only eighteen months, though they'd been sweethearts since high school.

Would Jane's marriage to Gage have been more successful if they hadn't gotten married so quickly, while they'd still been in college, where they'd met?

She rubbed her forehead again and set down the picture frame.

Melancholy. She hated it.

Annoyed with herself, she started up the computer and drank down half of the water while waiting for it to chug to life. For the past year, ever since she'd made the mistake of asking him for a little help with the recalcitrant thing, Casey had been after her to let him upgrade her system.

And you've only resisted because you wanted to do it yourself. He wanted to take over, and you balked.

During that first consultation, instead of fixing the computer, somehow or other, they'd ended up having sex in the storeroom after Colbys was closed down for the night.

She set the water bottle aside and thumped her hand on the side of the computer, pushing away the memory. The computer gave out a little hiccupping sound and a fan somewhere inside it whirred to life. A few moments later, the screen finally lit up, and she set about updating her books. It didn't take her long, because she kept up with the task almost daily even though she detested it. It might be overkill—her accountant, her ex-husband *and* Casey had all independently accused her of it—but she liked knowing to the penny where she was at any given time.

She used to think it came from watching her mother scrimp and save and worry about every dime right up until she died before Jane moved to Weaver. But Julia had come out of their childhood without sharing this particular obsession of Jane's.

"Pregnant yet?"

Startled, she swiveled in her chair, knocking the water bottle into the computer keyboard with her elbow. She gave Casey an annoyed look as she hastily yanked the keyboard off the desk, trying to protect it from the spilled water. "Ever hear of knocking?"

"Door wasn't closed." He was leaning casually against the doorjamb. "Wouldn't worry too much about that keyboard. It's already a decade past its life expectancy."

She used the hem of her sweater to swipe up the spreading puddle with one hand and held the keyboard aloft with the other. It was awkward because of the cords tethering it in place; though she'd never admit it, she wished she had the nifty wireless things that Casey had tried to equip her with. "What are you doing here?"

"Grabbing a bite."

The grill usually closed at ten on weeknights and it was still well before that. "Then get to it," she said waspishly. "Jerry's cooking alone tonight." During their busier times, her main cook was joined by his son, Jerry Junior.

Casey sighed noisily and grabbed the keyboard out of her hand, holding it high when she tried to take it back. "There's no crime in asking for help."

"I don't need help. I need a towel." More annoyed with the way her stomach was jumping around at the sight of him than she was the minor spill, she scooted past him and grabbed a neatly folded towel from a stack of them in the storeroom. It was only a matter of seconds, but when she reentered the office, he was already sitting down in her chair, boots propped on the corner of her desk while he tapped away at the keyboard resting on his lap.

"Stop that!" She tried shoving at his legs, but he was immovable. There was no room to get around him, so she reached across him to wipe the towel over the desktop, drying what was left of the water. She didn't have the computer hooked up to an internet connection—another source of contention between them—nor did she have any little computer games to amuse him. She needed the computer for one thing and one thing only: keeping her business records. "You're snooping."

"Nope." His fingers flew over the keyboard with enviable ease. "Just doing a little maintenance. When's the last time you backed up your data?"

She glared at the back of his head, controlling the urge to swat him with the towel even though it was mighty tempting. "Last week," she lied.

He snorted. "Last month, you mean." He tapped some more. "You need to be on an automatic backup. You're maxing out your memory. You won't let me add more. You keep everything that's important about Colbys on this thing." He looked over his shoulder up at her. "If you're not careful, you could lose it all."

He was the only person she'd ever met who had honest-to-goodness gray eyes. If she hadn't spent as many hours in his arms as she had, she would have suspected the distinctive color came from contact lenses rather than nature. But she was the one whose imperfect vision required the aid of contact lenses, not Casey.

His eyebrow rose and she realized she was standing there like an idiot, staring into his eyes. "Fine," she agreed abruptly. "I'll get a new computer. Update it all." She barely waited a beat. "*I* will get it," she emphasized. "I don't need you doing it for me."

"I swear, if you needed your own appendix taken out, you'd insist on holding the scalpel." He turned his attention back to the computer. "Still amazes me that you're willing to let someone else contribute their gene pool to this kid you want."

"You're just annoyed because I'm not letting you take over and do whatever *you* want."

He glanced at her again and sudden heat slid through her veins at the look in his eyes. "A month might have passed since you announced your little 'plan—'" he air-quoted the word "—but I'm pretty sure there're a few things I do that you still want, Janie."

She exhaled noisily and tossed the towel over his head. "Cool your jets, Clay." Because it was her own jets she was worried about, she backed out of the small office and headed out front to the bar. He wouldn't say or do anything in front of other people that would give any hint they were lovers.

Had been lovers, she mentally corrected herself.

Past tense.

Merilee was mixing up a round of frozen margaritas when Jane moved behind the bar. The noise of the blender was familiar and welcome. There were a few orders waiting, and she tied a black apron around her hips, then washed her hands before starting to fill them.

Casey appeared soon after but rather than going over to the grill as she expected, he slid onto one of the bar stools near where she was working. "Think I'll eat in here," he said.

She wanted to gnash her teeth. Instead, without missing a beat on the Long Island iced tea she was concocting, she slid a menu in front of him.

He flipped the laminated card between his fingers. "I've got this thing memorized," he pointed out.

"Which only proves the fact that you spend too much time in a bar. Beer?"

He nodded. "You're the proprietress of said bar. I wouldn't complain about having regular customers if I were you. Bad for business."

She topped off the cocktail with a dash of cola, then moved down to the taps and drew his beer. She set the mug in front of him. "What's it going to be? No, wait. Let me guess. Meat loaf and mashed or the bacon cheeseburger with onion rings?"

"Janie." He gave her a lazy grin. "I'm touched. You know me so well."

"I know you never order a steak when you're here," she said drily.

"Considering my family's Double-C beefsteaks are the best around, why would I pay someone else for one?" He suddenly stretched across the bar toward her, but only to stick the menu back on the little pile beneath the bar.

She was glad she'd managed to control the urge to take a step back. "So which is it? Meat loaf or burger?"

"Spaghetti and meatballs."

She shrugged. "You're just saying that to be contrary, but it makes no difference to me. You're the one who'll regret it." She turned to the register and punched in the order, then started loading glasses into a dishwasher tray.

"Where's the fishbowl?"

Something in his tone made her neck prickle. She glanced at him. He wasn't smiling, but there was a definite smirk of amusement lurking in his gray eyes.

"I put it away."

"No takers in the win-a-date-with-Janie contest?"

"Actually, I had more entries than I knew what to do with. But I didn't need them after I met Keith. You must know him from Cee-Vid. Keith Lambert?" She folded her arms on the bar top and leaned toward him conspiratorially. "He's the perfect candidate. Intelligent. And that bow tie." She smiled slowly. "Once that comes off, he's very…energetic."

Casey's eyes narrowed. "I know you better than that, sport. Max isn't going to find Keith's body cut into pieces and left on the side of the road somewhere, is he? I'd hate to have to bail you out of jail."

Max was Max Scalise, the sheriff and Casey's cousin by marriage. There were times when Jane speculated that one out of every three people in Weaver was somehow related to the wealthy Clay family. "Why would I want to get rid of Keith?" Just because he was duller than dishwater? "He could turn out to be the—"

"Next Mr. Janie?"

"—man of my dreams."

Casey's lips twitched as he twisted his beer mug against the wooden surface of the bar. "In *his* dreams, maybe. A little young for you, isn't he?"

Jane looked up from his hand. Why was it that his hands were callused, suntanned and very masculine, when Keith's had been white as snow and softer than hers? The two men did the same sort of work, for Pete's sake.

Olive, one of the servers from the grill, arrived with his order of spaghetti and meatballs. She was nineteen and made quite a production over setting the plate in front of him, along with a napkin-wrapped set of flatware and a heaping helping of nubile come-hither smiles on the side.

"Thank ya, darlin'," Casey drawled.

Olive looked ready to swoon as she went through the archway back to the restaurant.

Jane pulled off her apron and set Casey's bill beside his plate. "A little young for you, isn't *she*?"

He laughed soundlessly. "Say the word, sport, and we can go right back to the way things were."

Fortunately, where he was concerned, she'd had lots of practice overlooking the way he made her stomach lurch, so she was reasonably confident she didn't display the same besotted expression as Olive.

"Oh, yeah?" She angled her head and batted her lashes comically. "You gonna put a ring on it and donate some genetic material?" She patted his cheek dismissively and walked away before she had to witness his response.

"Merilee," she called as she headed toward the exit, "make sure Casey Clay doesn't skip out on his bill. Don't want anyone around here thinking they can get things for free."

Casey watched Jane sail through the door, then glanced at Merilee, who was giving him a wry look.

"Think she had another bad date," Merilee shared, moving down to his end of the bar.

Casey would bet on it. But he could play ignorant when he wanted. He twirled his fork in the spaghetti noodles. "What makes you say that?"

Merilee grinned. She was a little younger than Jane and lived over in Braden. Casey'd heard somewhere that she was engaged to a fireman. "If *you* had a good dinner date, would you be hanging around your workplace an hour after appetizers?" She poured herself a cup of coffee and shook her head. "Not me, my friend. How's that pasta?"

"Not as good as the meat loaf would have been."

Merilee grinned. "Not one of Jerry's best dishes, that's for sure. Jane's been trying to get him to use her recipe, but he says the kitchen's his domain and unless she wants him to quit, to leave him to it."

Casey figured the only reason Jane allowed Jerry any leeway at all was because she couldn't easily replace him. When it came to her business, like her personal life, she wanted to control every damn little detail.

He didn't begrudge her that particular right—he called plenty of his own shots, too—but it definitely made dealing with her a challenge. "You said *another* bad date." He gave up on the watery spaghetti and bullet-hard meatballs and picked up the beer. It was just the way he liked. A little dark. A little toasty. And not too heavy on the hops. "She having a lot of 'em?"

Merilee obviously saw nothing odd in the question. There was a reason why gossip was Weaver's number-one sport. Everyone talked about everyone. "I know she's had a date every Thursday night for the past month with a different guy each time. Far as I can tell, none of them led to a second date. The rest of the time, she's here working."

He did have to give Jane props for being a hard worker. She might bust his chops about getting called into Cee-Vid at all hours, but she wasn't much better.

It was a good thing they'd never tried moving their relationship out of the bedroom. Even if she'd never been struck with baby fever, it still would have been a recipe for disaster.

Knowing it didn't make the thought particularly welcome, though.

"You can take that away," Casey told Merilee, nudging the still-full plate toward her.

"Want me to get you something else?"

He shook his head as he slid off the bar stool. He drained the last mouthful of beer and pulled some cash from his wallet that he dropped on the check. "Catch ya later, Merilee."

She scooped up the money with a smile and turned to the register. He left the bar and headed toward his truck, parked in the lot that was situated between Colbys and the dance studio.

Even at that hour of the evening, there was still activity over there. Business was obviously going well for his cousin.

He drove out of the lot but was too restless to head home. He briefly considered dropping by his parents' place. Maggie and Daniel Clay still lived in the house where Casey had been born and raised. But he decided against it. He enjoyed his folks' company, but he wasn't in the mood for a dose of happy hearth and home. For the same reason, he didn't drop by J.D.'s place. His sister and her husband, Jake, were always welcoming, too. Jake's twin boys—preteen hellions that they were—would be chasing around while two-year-old Tucker did his level best to keep up with his big brothers.

He rubbed his fingers absently over the gnawing in his chest and drove without stopping right past his own house—a hundred-and-twenty-year-old farmhouse that he'd moved from the country into town and restored with his dad's help—all the way to Shop-World, which was on the other side of Weaver.

His excuse was he needed to pick up some groceries for his empty refrigerator. That Janie lived out by the big-box store was just a coincidence.

Her bright and shiny silver pickup was parked in front of her condo when he trolled past. She'd turned on her porch light. He looked up at the still-dark window on the second floor directly above the door. Her bedroom. He doubted she'd gone to bed. She was probably puttering around in her kitchen or the walled-in yard she had out back, where he'd always parked before when he'd come calling. It was rare for her to just sit and chill. She always seemed to need to be doing something.

He circled the block, giving up the pretense altogether that he cared about groceries when he passed Shop-World for the second time without a glance, and slowly drove past her condo again. The light had gone on in her bedroom window, and she was standing in front of the window looking out.

Dammit.

No way she'd fail to see his dusty black pickup truck creeping, two miles an hour, down her street when there was a big ol' streetlamp overhead. Speeding up would make him look even more stupid. Stopping altogether wasn't an option.

She wanted things he couldn't give her, he reminded himself.

Then she lifted her arms and closed the white plantation shutters, cutting herself off from view.

Another needless reminder. She wanted things, but not from him.

His jaw tight, he turned around and drove home.

Chapter Four

"Arlo Bellamy."

Jane turned her attention from the strawberry daiquiris she was mixing for a trio of young women she'd just carded to Hayley, who was sitting at the end of the bar. "What?"

Hayley tucked her hair behind her ear. She was nodding. "Arlo Bellamy. I don't know why I didn't think of him before. He's my neighbor. You should go out with him."

Despite herself, Jane's gaze flicked toward the pool tables.

It was Saturday night and the Clay contingent was out in force. Casey was there, wielding his personal pool cue with his typical expertise. He had at least a dozen relatives with him. With a group that large, she would have assumed they were celebrating something special. But experience had already shown her that when it came to the Clay family, they didn't seem to need any special reason to socialize en masse.

"He's thirty-eight," Hayley was saying. "He's the estate lawyer who has that office down on Second Street."

Jane focused with an effort on her friend's voice rather than Casey. "The one who has that bronze horse statue out in front?"

Hayley nodded. "I think you'd have a lot in common."

"Never met him." She couldn't recall the lawyer ever stepping foot in Colbys.

"So? He's nice."

"How do you know? Just because he's a lawyer?" She flipped on the blender and assembled three glasses in front of her. "Guy could be a stalker." She thought of Casey driving past her house the other evening.

She'd been dangerously close to beckoning him to come inside.

And where would that have gotten her?

Certainly no closer to marriage and a baby.

"I doubt he's a stalker," Hayley said drily. "He'd have chosen to live somewhere other than Weaver where he'd have a larger pool of pickings."

Jane killed the blender and poured out the sweet drinks. Personally, she found the daiquiri concoctions sickening, but they never failed to appeal to a good portion of her patrons. She swirled whipped cream on top of the pink drinks and set them on a tray for her server to pick up, then started on the next order. She'd been tending bar for so many years that the motions were routine. Comfortable. "If he's so nice, why haven't you dated him?"

Hayley gave her a look. "Girlfriend, *you* are the one who says she's on the hunt for a husband. Not me."

"Nor me," Sam Dawson said as she stepped up to the

bar and slid onto the stool that Hayley had been saving
for her. "Sorry I'm late."

Unconcerned, Hayley waved her hand toward Jane.
"You've met Arlo," she said to Sam. "Tell her he's a nice
guy."

"He's a nice guy," Sam said obediently. Her dark blond
hair was pulled into the usual knot at the back of her
head. "No arrests since I've been here."

Hayley grinned. "See, Jane? No arrests."

Jane set a bottle of light beer in front of Sam and
flipped off the bottle cap in the same motion before turning back to her order. "High praise, all right." She wondered if Casey had ever been arrested.

Probably not. From all appearances, as a general rule
the Clays seemed to be a highly upstanding lot.

"Arlo might not want to go out with me, then." She
pulled the bottle of Grey Goose down from the shelf behind her and poured it liberally over ice. "I have been."
She followed the vodka with a splash of freshly squeezed
grapefruit juice and set the drink on another tray. For
whatever reason, cocktails seemed to be the order of the
evening among the crowd. Usually beer and margaritas
were the heavy favorites but that night she was serving
up everything from Manhattans to Slippery Nipples.

"No way." Both Hayley and Sam looked agog.

She paused in front of them, long enough to pull another steaming rack of glasses out of the dishwasher.
"That's how I met Gage in college. A couple dozen of
us were protesting the unfair firing of a professor and
we all got picked up." She set the rack on the rubberized
mat next to the small sink and moved down to the taps.
"Eventually, the charges were dismissed."

A burst of laughter came from the crowd of Clays surrounding the pool tables, drawing more eyes than just

Jane's. Which was fortunate for her, because she had no witnesses to the way she managed to spill Guinness over her hand while she watched Casey's fine, fine behind as he leaned over for his shot. She shut off the tap and swiped her hand over her apron, then loaded up another tray. She had three cocktail waitresses on hand that night, and they were stretched to the max. Pulling someone over from the restaurant wasn't an option. Every table there was full, too, with a line of people stretching out the door, waiting.

A fine October night in Weaver. The weather was good, no snow yet, and people were out for a good time.

Rather than let the orders keep stacking up, she stepped out from behind the bar and delivered several herself and collected quite a few empties on her way back. Some young guy was trying to chat up Hayley and Sam, and her friends looked amused and happily occupied.

Everything was exactly as she'd planned when Gage had given her the money five years ago to buy Colbys, and she couldn't help smiling to herself as she went behind the glossy wood bar again and pulled up the next order.

One root beer. One designer microbrew that she ordered from Montana. The microbrew that she'd begun carrying only because it was Casey's favorite.

The combination was what Casey and his cousin Erik usually ordered and she figured now was no exception. She glanced over at the pool tables. Only this time, instead of seeing Casey's rear end, she saw him leaning against the wall, staring boldly back at her.

Heat shot through her, and she tore her gaze away from his. She pulled out an icy bottle of root beer along with a frosted mug, filled another with Casey's beer and stuck them on a tray before going back over to her girlfriends.

She had a plan and she was sticking to it.

"Give your neighbor my number," she told Hayley. She had to raise her voice, because the jukebox was blaring, billiard balls were clacking, and the crowd gave off a general blur of chatter and laughter.

Hayley's eyebrows lifted. She glanced from Jane's face across the room toward the pool tables. Then she nodded.

Satisfied, Jane washed her sticky hands and reached for the next order.

She didn't allow herself any more glances toward the pool tables and the very unreachable Casey Clay.

Even though Casey saw Jane play server several times, she didn't play server to his party. And when he was called into work just before ten o'clock, he was glad for the excuse to escape. Glad, at least, until he got to his office and spent the next twelve hours studying satellite feeds and reports regarding three agents who'd gone missing in Central America.

By the next night, the situation had escalated even more, and the next thing he knew, he found himself sitting beside Tristan on a plane to Hollins-Winword's headquarters in Connecticut.

Four days later, he was watching two caskets being carried off a plane while rain poured down on their heads.

"This isn't your fault." Tristan stood next to him on the tarmac, looking as grim as Casey had ever seen.

"Feels like it," Casey returned flatly. "I was the last one in communication with them."

"And their status was still clear," Tristan pointed out.

"Was still my watch," he said. It didn't matter that there'd been others on shift, as well. Casey was their commander. He was supposed to be the one who could find a gnat on a wall eight thousand miles away.

"At least we had something to recover. There was a time we wouldn't have even been able to retrieve their bodies." Tristan's boss, Coleman Black, stood on the other side of Casey. Coleman was a hard-looking older man with gray hair and a face lined from sun and responsibility. The only time Casey had ever seen him really smile had been on the rare occasions he was around Casey's sister Angeline and her husband, Brody Paine. Casey's brother-in-law was Cole's son—a rarely acknowledged fact because of the inherent dangers that went along with that—and his visits were extremely rare; Casey could count them on one hand.

But in his role with Hollins-Winword, Casey had had many more encounters with the agency's head.

"Back when your uncle here was a young buck," Cole was saying, "we wouldn't have been able to do a lot of the things we can now." He shook his head as they watched the caskets being loaded into a waiting black hearse.

"Jefferson'd be the first to confirm that," Tristan murmured.

Tristan's older brother Jefferson had been an HW field agent back in the day. During an especially tricky assignment, he'd landed in a third-world prison; ultimately, he'd escaped, but his partner hadn't. Even though Jefferson had returned to Weaver to become a horse breeder, had gotten married, had two grown kids and an ever-growing herd of grandchildren, the experience all those years ago still colored his life. When his son, Axel, had followed in his footsteps with the agency, he had *not* been particularly thrilled.

"We should've been able to do more," Casey said now. Failure. Grief. Responsibility. It all weighed inside his gut like concrete blocks holding him below water. "Kept those caskets from ever being needed, and we damn sure should've found McGregor by now." The third part of the missing trio was still a big fat unknown. They didn't know if Jason McGregor's body was lying in a ditch somewhere, tossed aside the same way Jon and Manny had been. They didn't know squat.

"It's not your fault," Tristan said again. "You've got to have something to go on and we're flying blind."

Cole made a sound Casey figured was meant to be agreement, though with the cagey old guy, it was hard to tell. He clapped Casey once on the shoulder before letting out a sigh and walking out from beneath the shelter of the airplane hangar into the rain toward the hearse.

"He's going along to meet the families," Tristan said.

"Will he tell them the truth about how they died?"

His uncle's lips twisted and he shook his head. "If he follows his own protocol? No. But it never pays to anticipate Cole's actions too much. The man's a law unto himself."

He turned and gave Casey a long look. Even though Casey was tall, his uncle still topped him by an inch. "I've been in your shoes, Case," he reminded him. "I was never in the field either. Stayed safe, closed up in an office miles—usually countries—away from the action. But we're supposed to be the guardian angels, making sure those guys taking their chances out there in the field make it safely back home again. And I know only too well that it's not easy to handle when that doesn't happen."

"I want to know what went wrong," Casey muttered. "I want to find McGregor."

"We will. We'll investigate."

"I know. And I also know that not every investigation bears fruit."

The hearse, with Cole inside, drove away. The private airfield where the plane had landed was once again empty.

"Take my advice." Tristan nudged him back toward the black SUV in which they'd arrived. "Go back home. Put your arms around that pretty bartender of yours—"

Startled, Casey shot him a look. "*What*?"

"You're Hollins-Winword, kid," Tristan drawled, looking vaguely amused. "Nephew of mine or not, you know what that means. There's nothing in your life that you're going to keep secret from us." He climbed behind the wheel of the SUV himself, having dismissed the driver he'd been assigned even before they'd left HW's headquarters.

Casey got in the passenger seat and pinched the bridge of his nose, willing away the headache that was forming. "Secrets aside, she's anything but *mine*."

"Most of us start out thinking that way." His uncle drove out from beneath the hangar and headed in the opposite direction the hearse had taken. "Regardless, I'm telling you to focus on something good. Don't take the crap that happened here home to bed with you. When they went off grid, you did everything anyone could have done to find them. You can't control from a distance what those guys do once they're on an op. That buck doesn't stop at your door." His hands tightened around the steering wheel and he sighed. "It stops with Cole. And he's been dealing with that reality since before you were a sparkle in your daddy's eye. McGregor is good in the field. If he's able to lift his head, we'll find him. Bring him back safely. But in the meantime, you've got to let go of the things you can't change or you're going to end up useless. Not just to the agency but to everyone who cares about you outside of the agency, as well."

It was probably the longest speech he'd ever heard from his uncle. "Easier said than done."

"I know." Tristan waited a few beats. "Your bartender—"

"She's not—"

"*The* bartender, then," Tristan fired back. "What's the problem there?"

Casey hadn't discussed this particular situation with anyone. Not Erik. Not even his own father. But Tris wasn't his father. He was his boss. His mentor. "She wants to get married."

"Then put a ring on her finger already," his uncle said as if the answer were obvious. "You've been sleeping with her for more than a year, for God's sake."

Casey felt his neck get hot like some kid called on the carpet. He stared out at the Connecticut countryside. HW's compound—hidden in plain sight—was located inside a toilet-paper factory. "She doesn't want to marry *me*. She was plenty clear about it."

His uncle waited a beat. "And you believed her?" He sounded as if he wanted to laugh and Casey looked over at him. "Son, you have a lot to learn about women."

Casey grimaced. "It doesn't matter anyway. She only wants a husband so she can have a baby."

Tristan's eyebrow lifted. "So?"

"I'm not interested," he said flatly, and looked out the side window again, ending the conversation.

But it seemed that there were some things the omniscient Hollins-Winword didn't know after all.

Because even if Casey was interested in making a baby with Janie Cohen, he was incapable of it.

Thanks to a case of the mumps while he'd been doing a semester of college in Europe, he was sterile.

And there wasn't one damn thing he could do to change it.

* * *

"So, Jane." Arlo smiled down at her as they stood on her front porch. "I hope you enjoyed yourself this evening as much as I did."

Jane squelched the pang inside her. Arlo was a perfectly attractive guy. He was intelligent. Well-read. Humorous. He hadn't talked about an ex-girlfriend all night. He had no ex-wives. No baggage at all from previous relationships. He had insisted on paying for their dinner—Chinese—at the restaurant they'd gone to in Braden. His car had been spotless inside, he wore a suit and tie with comfort, and he even had a full head of brown hair.

And most of all, he'd talked about how—now that he was well established in his career—he'd realized there were things missing in his life that he wanted.

Like a wife.

A family.

He couldn't have more perfectly matched her requirements if he'd tried.

"I had a very nice time, Arlo."

He smiled and kissed her cheek. "So when I call you tomorrow, you'll answer?"

She couldn't help smiling. He didn't make her bells and whistles ring—*yet*, she made herself add—but he was exactly what Hayley had said. A nice man. "Yes, I'll answer."

His eyes crinkled a little as his smile widened. His teeth were white and perfectly straight. Then he pushed open the door that she'd unlocked. "Until tomorrow, then."

"Until tomorrow." She waited in the doorway, watching him until he reached his sedate Volvo. In a community dominated by pickup trucks and SUVs, his choice of a sedan certainly set him apart. He sketched a wave before climbing in and driving off.

She let out a sigh and slowly stepped into her house and closed the door.

"Thought good ol' Arlo was never gonna leave."

She screeched and threw her keys at where the voice was coming from before it penetrated that Casey was the one speaking. She pressed her hand to her racing heart and leaned forward slightly, feeling a little dizzy from the fright.

But then she snapped up, straight as a board, and glared at him. "What the *hell* are you doing here?"

He was sprawled on her couch, looking way too much at home in his worn jeans, ugly red shirt with cartoonish fish swimming across it and cowboy boots. "Waiting for you, obviously."

She closed her eyes and counted to ten. When she opened them again, he was still there. Messy butterscotch hair, gray eyes and all. She tried again. "How did you get in?" she asked with what she considered to be extraordinary patience.

"You left your back door open." He pulled his boots off the arm of her couch and sat up. "You ought to be more careful, sport. No point in locking the front door if you ignore the back one. You never know what sort of trouble you might be inviting."

"Weaver's as safe as a church," she muttered crossly. She dropped her purse on the glass coffee table in front of the couch and tossed her lightweight wool coat on the armchair. "Turns out you're the only trouble I needed to worry about. Do I need to count the silver?"

His lips curved but the amusement didn't seem to quite make it to his eyes. "What sort of grade did Arlo earn?"

"An A," she said crisply. "Plus."

"Liar. I saw that tepid cheek kiss he gave you."

"So not only do you break and enter, but you spy, as well."

"Door totally unlocked," he repeated. "A regular invitation, I figure. If you were really interested in Arlo, you'd have invited him in."

"And we'd have found you squatting in my living room. How were you planning to explain that?"

He shrugged. "I knew you wouldn't invite him in."

She snorted. "You knew nothing of the sort." She strode into the kitchen and pulled a half-empty bottle of chardonnay out of the refrigerator. Arlo, it turned out, was a teetotaler. Which she completely respected. Even though she owned a bar and grill, she wasn't much of a drinker. But finding Casey in her house was more than she could take.

She grabbed a glass from her cupboard, wiped the dust out of it and poured the wine. She took a fortifying gulp, then carried it with her back to the living room. She pointed her finger at him. "Do I need to call the sheriff on you?"

He pulled out his cell phone and handed it to her. "Max is on my speed dial," he offered, annoyingly helpful. "All of my cousins are."

She exhaled noisily and collapsed on the other end of the couch. "Casey—"

"I just wanted to see you."

She slowly closed her mouth, absorbing that. Her fingers tightened around the glass. She could have offered him one. He'd been the one to introduce her to that particular winery in the first place. The first time she'd invited him to her place after they'd moved their relationship into the "benefits" category, he'd brought a bottle of wine.

She'd been wholly unnerved by it and told him they

weren't dating—just mutually filling a need—and to save the empty romantic gestures.

He hadn't brought a bottle of wine ever again.

She shook off the memory.

He was here now, in her home, uninvited, and she'd be smart to remember that. "Why?"

He pushed off the couch and prowled around her living room. He'd always been intense. But she'd never really seen him *tense*. And she realized she was seeing it now.

She slowly sat forward and set her glass on the coffee table, watching him. "Casey, what's wrong?"

He shoved his fingers through his hair, not answering. Instead, he stopped in front of a photo collage on the wall above her narrow bookcase that Julia had given her last Christmas. "You going to go out with him again?"

Something ached inside her. "Probably," she admitted after a moment.

"He's a good guy," he muttered. "A little straitlaced, but otherwise okay."

She didn't know what was going on with him. But she suddenly felt like crying, and Jane wasn't a person who cried. "Casey."

"You could do worse." Then he gave her a tight smile and walked out of the living room into the kitchen. A second later, she heard the sound of her back door opening and closing.

He couldn't have left her more bewildered if he'd tried.

Chapter Five

An hour later, she was no closer to understanding what had happened.

She tried to finish her wine.

Couldn't.

She tried to read the suspense novel by her favorite author that she'd recently ordered.

Couldn't.

She removed her contacts and changed out of the dress she'd worn for her date with Arlo and into her softest, oldest T-shirt, hoping to relax enough to sleep.

Couldn't.

The one thing she could do, it turned out, was pull on a pair of sweatpants and fuzzy-lined clogs, grab her wallet and keys and head out.

She might never have been inside Casey's house before—always preferring to keep things on her turf—but she knew where it was located and less than fifteen minutes later, she was idling in front of a big farmhouse.

Out of curiosity, she'd driven by his place once. Okay. Twice. Well…half a dozen times. But only because it was on her way to Hayley's house. If Jane drove a little out of her way.

And she thought now, as she always did, that the farmhouse ought to have looked out of place—with its white clapboard siding, black shutters and steeply pitched roofs—situated there on the wide, tree-lined residential street rather than in the middle of a farm somewhere. But it didn't. A person could have fit about a half-dozen dwellings the size of her condo on the grassy lot that surrounded the two-storied white house. The entire place looked timeless. And pristine.

And it was just one more piece of the puzzle that was Casey Clay. The king of no commitment owned a house that looked made for family. Generations of them.

She turned into the long stone-paved driveway running up to and alongside the house, where his truck was sitting in front of a large detached garage. She parked behind him, dropped her keys in the empty cup holder molded into her console and got out of her truck.

Now that she was here, she was beset with nerves.

What if he told her to leave?

Yes, they'd always gone to her condo when they'd wanted to be alone together. She'd insisted on it, wanting to keep everything on her terms. And he'd never argued. He was no more interested in having their encounters dissected and discussed by the thriving Weaver grapevine than she.

Now, though, she couldn't help thinking that he'd been so agreeable to her terms because he actually hadn't *wanted her* in his personal space.

She nudged up her glasses, annoyed with herself, and firmly shut the truck door. Ignoring the *rat-a-tat* of her heart inside her chest and her goose bumps from the chilly night air, she strode around to the front of the house, her shoes snapping against the soles of her sock-less feet. She darted up the wooden steps, which were warmly illuminated by two lights framing the black door, and lifted her hand to knock.

But the mournful wail of a violin coming from in-side the house stopped her knuckles from connecting with the door.

The strain of music was pure and haunting.

And it was the saddest sound she'd ever heard.

Instead of knocking, she pressed her palm flat against the door and realized she was barely breathing as she lis-tened with only the two old-fashioned rocking chairs that furnished the wooden porch for company.

How much more was there about him that she didn't know?

Suddenly, the music cut off and a mighty crash vi-brated through the door and her palm.

Her heart shot into her throat and she instinctively turned the doorknob. It was unlocked, so she shoved open the door, rushing inside too quickly to appreciate the warm wood floor, the creamy white walls or the wide staircase opening onto the entry. "Casey?"

Silence weighed through the house as soon as she called out his name.

She dropped her wallet on a multidrawered chest sit-ting against the wall and headed farther into the house, passing a room on her left that was empty except for a single ladder-back chair and a small powder room on the right. "Casey?"

He suddenly appeared in the hallway ahead of her. He was shirtless, wearing only the jeans that he'd had on earlier when he'd invaded her house. "What are you doing here, Jane?"

Her mouth went a little dry. She wasn't sure if it was because of the spectacular washboard abs that never failed to amaze her, the unfamiliar dark frown on his face or the fact that he'd just called her Jane—not Janie, not sport, not darlin', not any of the dozens of nicknames he had for her.

"I heard a noise," she said, her voice oddly husky. "I was worried. Are you all right?"

His lips were tight. Thin. The lines of his carved jaw sharper than ever. "Go home."

The words sliced through her. Painfully. More painfully than they should have, considering her choice to end things with him. And she very nearly turned around and left.

Until she saw the line of blood trickling down his arm.

She stiffened her spine and closed the gap between them. "No."

His gaze darkened as she reached him. She looked from the deep scratch on his forearm up to his face, then beyond his tall, broad form to the room behind him. Interior walls had obviously been removed at some point, because she was fairly certain that farmhouses such as his weren't originally built to have great rooms. But that was what she was looking at. A huge open space dominated by tall windows and furnished with leather furniture, a long plank-top dining room table and a state-of-the-art kitchen.

Not even her self-made ex-husband had a house like it, and Gage—a real estate developer—was loaded.

She looked past all of that, though, and focused on the bookshelf that was toppled on its side, surrounded by scattered books and broken glass.

The violin on top of that mess, though, was the worst. A mangled mess of strings and fractured wood.

Casey was six and a half feet of unwelcoming hard muscle standing in her path, but she moved around him, walking over to the destruction. Glass crunched beneath her shoes as she reached down and carefully picked up the violin. The neck was broken in two. Only one string kept it tethered to the rest of the body.

Cradling the wounded instrument in both hands, she looked at him. "Were you *playing* this?" When she'd heard the music, she'd assumed he was merely listening to it. Not creating it.

He didn't answer, though. "You're going to cut yourself."

"Like you did?" She stepped out of the field of broken glass and gently set the violin on the granite island that stood between the bank of staggered kitchen cupboards and the eye-catching long table. She lifted one foot, then the other, looking to see if there was any glass stuck in the rubbery soles of her clogs. She didn't see any and she went around the far side of the island, putting it between them.

His dark frown had grown to a scowl and she wasn't sure if he was about to physically march her right out the front door.

"Where's your first-aid stuff?"

He just glared.

"Okay. How about your broom?" He wasn't any more forthcoming about that, so she started opening doors that might conceivably be hiding one. She found a walk-in pantry that was mostly empty except for several rolls of paper towels and a gigantic stack of paper plates. But no broom. She edged closer to him and opened another door. It revealed a staircase going down to a basement.

"Jane."

She quickly opened the last tall cupboard and gratefully snatched out the long-handled broom stowed inside. Giving him a wide berth, she rounded the island again and started sweeping up the glass. "At least wash out that scratch."

"I don't want you here."

She sucked down the sting. "Yup. I get that loud and clear." Sweep, sweep, sweep. His wood floors were stained a gray ashy color that was spectacularly striking. "Wash it anyway."

Watching him from the corners of her eyes, she saw his wide shoulders move restlessly. He yanked out one of the stools sitting against the island and sat on it, facing away from her. Then he clawed his fingers through his hair.

She chewed the inside of her cheek. Part of her wanted to go to him. Put her arms around him and press his head comfortingly against her breasts.

But that wasn't what they were about.

Her palms turned moist around the broom handle as she slowly gathered the shards of glass into a small pile.

His back was still toward her. He had a small scar over his right shoulder blade. She'd kissed her way over it dozens of times but had never asked what had caused it.

Why hadn't she asked?

Because she wasn't interested?

Or because she was afraid he wouldn't have told her?

She slowly propped the broom handle against the wall, leaving the bristles resting protectively over the pile of glass, and walked over to him. Her hand wasn't entirely steady when she placed it on his shoulder, but it was a lot steadier than her insides felt.

He stiffened at her touch and looked at her.

The scratch on his arm was deep enough to bleed, but up close she could see it had already stopped.

Her heart was thumping hard.

She didn't know what was tormenting him.

And maybe comfort wasn't their thing.

But she did know what was.

She leaned forward and slowly pressed her lips against his. She felt him inhale slightly. Resistance, almost.

But not quite.

She tilted her head a little and continued kissing him.

And after a moment, he lifted his hand and sank his fingers into the ponytail at the back of her head as he kissed her in return.

Suddenly, he tugged on her hair, pulling her head back until he could look into her face. She didn't know what he saw there. She didn't even know what she saw in his face, except the shadows behind those silvery-gray eyes. But he abruptly shifted and pulled her in front of him, lifting her onto the granite surface so fast that she didn't have a chance to even gasp.

He nudged her chin up with his thumb. His hooded gaze seemed to burn as he studied her. She swallowed hard when he slowly rubbed his thumb over her lower lip. She could hear her pulse pounding inside her head when his hand moved again, palm flattening as he ran it down her neck. Her chest. Fiery heat gathered along the path he took downward, her ancient T-shirt offering no protection whatsoever.

He reached her belly and kept on going, until cotton knit gave way to worn fleece.

Jane sucked in a sharp breath as his hand dragged down her abdomen. She had no resistance to offer when he slid his palm between her legs.

"Take off your glasses."

She moistened her lips at his low, gruff voice and set aside her glasses.

"Now your hair. Let it down."

She tugged the rubber band out of her hair and dropped it on the granite.

"Take off your shirt."

Her nerves lurched inside her.

She bunched the hem of her shirt in her damp fists and pulled it over her head. She wasn't wearing a bra. Hadn't bothered to put one back on before she'd driven over. Her nipples were so tight they ached, and when he leaned forward—no hesitation, no apology—and grazed his teeth over one, then swirled his tongue around it, she shuddered, arching involuntarily against his hand.

"Take off your sweats."

A soft sound she didn't recognize rose in her throat. Her hands shook as she pushed down the elastic waistband. She had to lean back on her elbows to lift her hips enough to get them down. Her shoes had long since fallen off her feet and she let the sweatpants slide off her legs. But before she could push up from her elbows and sit up, his hand flattened again between her breasts, his splayed fingers stretching from one nipple to the other. "Stay put."

She opened her mouth to protest. She wanted to put her hands on him. To run her fingers over every familiar ridge and hollow. To sink down on him, feel him filling her, blotting out everything else in the world.

But the protest didn't come. Instead, she quivered, unreasonably aroused by following his command, and stayed put.

His fingertips pressing into her, he slowly moved them down her belly again until they reached the elastic edge of her white bikini panties.

She pressed her lips together, her heart thundering as he dipped beneath the elastic, followed it around her hip, slid beneath her to cup her bottom.

"Lift."

She arched and he yanked the cotton down her thighs.

She bit back the weird cry that climbed up her throat. "Casey—"

"Don't say one word, Jane." His voice was little more than a rasp. "You started this."

She couldn't stop trembling. She *had* started this. She'd kissed him.

And now she was sprawled on display for him atop a cold granite expanse. He hadn't even taken off his jeans, though she could tell he was just as turned on as she was.

And she couldn't have stopped now if her life depended on it.

She exhaled audibly, and finally, his silvery gaze released hers, running down her body the same way that his hand had. Then, still sitting on the stool, he closed his hands over her hips and he dragged her closer and lowered his mouth onto her.

Her head fell back and she groaned as heat blasted through her. She grabbed his shoulders. His hair. Anything to steady herself, anything to keep her from spinning mindlessly out of control as his tongue stroked, teased and tormented. But there was no defense against him, against the tension spreading like wildfire inside her. And he knew it, for he gripped her harder, closer, tasted deeper, even more deliberately, and suddenly, the pleasure was too much to contain. It exploded from her pores, arching her sharply against his tethering hold as she cried out his name.

Casey exhaled roughly, deliberately gentling his grip on her smooth, creamy thighs before he left bruises. Her hands had fallen weakly to her sides. Her hair was a mass of blond curls spread across his counter, her chest rising and falling in time to her panting breath. The need to bury himself inside her was overwhelming. But he hung on to the last shred of resistance he possessed like a drowning man until, millimeter by millimeter, he was able to pull himself away from the drug that was Janie Cohen.

He pressed his mouth against the satiny flesh of her inner thigh and felt the shiver work through her. Then he pushed back, straightening painfully from the wooden bar stool.

He didn't look at her. Couldn't, or he'd chuck his common sense entirely out the window and carry her up to his bedroom and keep her there for an eternity.

He picked up the oversize faded blue T-shirt she'd been wearing and tossed it onto the counter next to the broken violin.

She closed her hand over the shirt, then bunched it against her waist. Her coffee-colored gaze followed him.

"Go home, Janie."

Her lips parted. Red came and went in her beautiful face. She pushed up on one elbow. Golden. Feminine. Naked. "I'm not leaving you like this."

Some corner of his mind thought that under other circumstances, that sentiment might have been funny coming from her.

"If you won't leave, then I will."

Her brow knit. She sat up all the way and yanked the shirt over her head, fumbled with her glasses, then jumped off the granite-topped island and pulled on the rest of her clothes with jerky motions. Her shoes clenched in one fist, she stopped in front of him.

Stared up at him through those damned sexy glasses.

"Clean out that scratch," she said tightly. "You might still have glass in it."

Then she stomped past him toward the front of the house.

A few seconds later, he heard the door slam behind her.

He exhaled, looked up at the ceiling and squeezed the back of his neck between his hands.

If he could strangle himself, he would.

At least then he'd be out of his misery.

"Stupid, stupid, stupid."

Jane was still muttering the words under her breath the next morning as she stocked the bar in preparation for another Friday night.

She didn't know if she was accusing herself of stupidity or *him*.

She knew it didn't matter, as she muscled a fresh beer keg into place in her cooler and connected it. Because the word fit them both.

To a capital-sized boldface *T*.

She closed the door to the cooler and returned to the front of the bar. She was needlessly mopping the floor that Merilee had already mopped the night before when the air around her seemed to turn thin.

She looked up to see Casey walking through from the restaurant.

Her hands clenched around the mop handle, but that only reminded her of sweeping up the glass at his place the night before. And where *that* had ended.

She propped the mop against the counter and folded her arms, giving him a cool stare. It wasn't often that she saw him dressed in something other than jeans and crazy shirts. Unless he was undressed, that was.

She shook off that annoying detail.

"You look dressed for a funeral," she greeted when he stopped on the other side of the bar. Black suit. White shirt and pale blue tie. Even his hair, usually too long, wavy and rumpled, was trimmed and brushed brutally back from his lean face.

His lips twisted. He dropped her wallet on the bar between them. "You left that at my place."

She flushed. In her rush to escape the night before, she hadn't even realized she'd forgotten it. She snatched it and shoved it inside a drawer full of Colbys drink coasters located on the shelves on the wall behind her.

When she turned back around, he was already departing again.

She stared after him until long after he was gone.

"Stupid, stupid, stupid," she muttered again.

Chapter Six

"Did you tell her where you're going?"

Casey shook his head at Tristan's question when he climbed into the SUV waiting in Colbys's parking lot. "No point."

He was glad his uncle refrained from sharing whatever it was he thought about that. Instead, they just settled in for the drive to the private airstrip Tris maintained outside of town, where a jet emblazoned with Cee-Vid on the side was waiting. It took them straight to Phoenix, where an air-conditioned town car drove them out to the National Cemetery. There, in the shade of an overhead awning that protected them from the glare of a merciless October sun though not the heat of it, they stood respectfully behind the seated family members burying their beloved son, Jonathan, who'd been a decorated marine before he'd ever heard of Hollins-Winword.

Cole, Casey knew, was attending another funeral, for

Manny, on the other side of the country in Maine. He couldn't be in both places, so Tristan—his second in command—got the task. Casey had threatened to go on his own until his uncle relented and said Casey could come with him.

As they stood there, listening to the uniformed minister offering the eulogy, Casey couldn't stop thinking about how Jon's family was completely ignorant of the life he had lived. Sharing those secrets voluntarily wouldn't have lessened their love. But learning of them involuntarily? If they ever discovered the magnitude of what their son had kept from them, would they see it as a betrayal? Or would they understand that such things were done in hopes of protecting them?

Even among his own family members, there were few who knew about Cee-Vid's secret.

The sharp report of the first rifle volley assaulted his ears, and he focused on the seven riflemen as they shot off two more rounds. Then they tucked several shell casings into the now tightly folded United States flag that had been draped over the casket.

A prayer. More tears as the flag was handed over to parents who'd never know the whole truth.

And it was done.

Even offering their condolences afterward had the gloss of lies. Yes, they were professional acquaintances of Jonathan's. No, they couldn't join the family for sandwiches and refreshing iced tea at their home later. Yes, Jon had had a hell of a sense of humor and a deeply ingrained sense of honor.

Then Tristan and Casey climbed back into the air-conditioned town car, which carried them back to the airport.

By nightfall they were in Weaver, where the temperatures were a good forty degrees colder, and the only thing that Casey wanted was a drink.

Of the alcoholic kind.

Going to Colbys, though, was about the last thing he wanted to do. Drinking at home, alone, was about the last thing he should be doing. It was what had led to him beating the hell out of the violin that had once belonged to his grandmother Sarah. She'd died giving birth to her youngest son, Tristan, and the only way that Casey's generation knew her at all was through their grandfather Squire.

If Squire ever learned what he'd done, the old man— ninety-something or not—would rightfully string Casey up by his heels.

Instead of going anywhere else, instead of drinking anything at all, he ended up seeking sanctuary in his office at Cee-Vid. But not even there, among his computers and monitors, where he used to feel most comfortable, did he find any peace.

Jane smoothed the edge of the banner she was hanging and fastened the last corner over the hook high on the wall above her shelves of liquor bottles. She glanced down at Hayley, who was sitting at the bar eating the grilled cheese sandwich she'd ordered for lunch. "Does it look straight to you?" From her angle, perched as she was on top of a ladder, Jane couldn't tell.

Hayley angled her head, studying the long rectangular banner. "Needs to come down a few inches on your side."

Jane adjusted it slightly, then, after Hayley's nod, climbed down from the ladder. She walked out into the middle of the room to get a look at the banner herself.

Each fall since she'd bought Colbys, Jane had sponsored a Halloween costume contest and toy drive in October and a food drive in November. But this was the first year she was adding a pool tournament in December, and she'd ordered a new banner advertising all the events at once. "Perfect." She went back behind the bar and folded the tall ladder to return it to the storeroom.

When she came back out again, Hayley had finished her sandwich and was stifling a yawn.

"Keeping you up?"

Hayley shook her head and smiled ruefully. "Sorry." Almost immediately, she hid another yawn behind her hand. "Out late last night dealing with an emergency."

"Sheriff's office call you in?" Jane knew Hayley was often called in by the sheriff's department when a situation required a counselor.

But Hayley shook her head again. "Spent half the night playing mediator to my own family members."

"Still in an uproar over your grandmother?"

"Archer warned me to keep my nose out of it."

Jane had met Hayley's older brother only once, when he'd come up from his home in Cheyenne to visit his sister. "I'm guessing that you didn't."

Hayley's lips twisted ruefully. "I invited her to come and stay with me."

"*Definitely* didn't keep your nose out of it." Jane automatically took away her friend's empty plate and refilled her water glass. "Is she going to?"

Hayley nodded. "Oh, yes. Vivian—I just can't get used to calling her *Grandma* when I don't even know her—is bound and determined to visit. She told my dad that she's coming whether he likes it or not. I couldn't very well let her stay in a motel. She'll be here this weekend."

Neither Braden nor Weaver possessed anything as fancy as an actual *hotel*. There were accommodations to be had—clean and decent—but by no means fancy. "And then what happens once she's here?"

"That is the hundred-dollar question." Hayley propped her chin on her hand and made a face. "If I knew the reasons why they were estranged in the first place, maybe I'd have a better idea."

"I'm sure you'll get to the bottom of it."

"Yes, but I have to admit I'm not used to navigating a minefield where my own family is concerned. It's a whole different ball of wax than doing so with my patients." She straightened and brushed her hands together as if mentally dismissing the matter. "Are you still getting any guff from the town council over adding another pool tournament?"

"Not too much anymore." They'd approved her event by a narrow margin, but it had still been approved. "I'm advertising all over the state and if the registrations are high enough, it'll just mean more tourism dollars during the town's tree-lighting celebration. They've already seen the dollars my July Fourth tournament has brought in for the town. Evidently, the idea of increasing their coffers was enough to silence the protests that we had no business holding a billiards tournament during the Christmas season." She shrugged. "Plus, the proceeds from the tournament are going to be split between the winners and local charities. They couldn't very well complain about that."

"Any registrations yet?"

"A few. But it's still early. I figure if I get even half of the crowd I get in July, it'll be a success."

"And will a certain gray-eyed man with the initials C and C be among them?"

Jane grabbed a handful of coasters from the drawer and stacked them neatly beneath the bar. She hadn't seen Casey in more than a week. Not since the morning he'd returned her wallet to her. "Can't imagine why not. He's always played before. Along with a passel of other members of the C family." The Clays were unfailingly supportive of community events. For Casey not to enter would imply there'd been more between them than just sex.

Since that clearly wasn't the case, she expected he'd play and finish as well as ever. He'd won the Fourth of July tournament the year before last.

She tapped the rounded edges of the stack again, neatening what didn't need neatening. "I, um, I told Arlo I'd go out with him again. Sunday afternoon." Tap, tap, tap. "There's some picnic thing going on in Braden with a bunch of his lawyer friends."

"Sounds like fun."

"It's nearly the end of October. It'll be too cold out for a picnic. I think I should cancel."

Hayley snorted softly. "Since when does a little cold bother you?"

She ignored that. "It's only Tuesday. He'll have plenty of time to find someone else to go with him."

"Thoughtful of you, though he might not agree. Why do you *really* want to cancel?"

Tap, tap, tap. Annoyed with herself, she moved the coasters out of her reach. She hadn't told Hayley what had happened when she'd gone to Casey's place. Hadn't told Hayley that she'd gone there at all.

Some things were simply too humiliating to share, even with your closest friend.

But she was afraid she'd agreed to Arlo's invitation as enthusiastically as she had only because she'd been so upset with Casey. And that wasn't at all fair to Arlo.

"Jane," Hayley prompted. "Why cancel?"

She gestured toward the banner. "Next to the summertime, I'm coming into my busiest time of year around here. I probably shouldn't be off gallivanting around at some park thirty miles away."

Hayley just smiled faintly and gave her a knowing look. "If you say so." Then she glanced at the oversize watch on her slender wrist. "I'd better get back to my office. I have patients this afternoon." She started to pay for her sandwich, but Jane waved off the money.

"You know that's no good here."

Hayley tucked away her wallet. "Far be it from me to turn down a free grilled cheese sandwich." She slid off the bar stool and glanced over her shoulder when the street-side door opened.

Sunshine streamed through the entrance, blocked only by the tall shape of Casey as he strolled inside, his shoulders looking more massive than ever thanks to the leather bomber jacket he was wearing.

Jane's mouth dried.

Casey's cousin Axel entered behind him, and they headed toward the pool tables.

Axel lifted a hand in a casual, easy greeting.

Casey didn't look her way at all.

"Have a good time on Sunday with Arlo," Hayley advised, loudly and cheerfully, before heading out the same door the men had just come through.

Jane felt her face flush when Casey finally looked her way at that.

She turned her back on him and started hanging a garland of Halloween pumpkins and white spiderwebs from the shelves behind her, but the tingling on the back of her neck told her when he came up to the bar. She schooled her expression and looked at him over her shoulder. "What'll it be? Usual?"

"It's barely past noon."

She turned to face him as if he were any other customer. "It's always five o'clock somewhere." She tossed a towel over her shoulder and managed to look at him without really looking at him. "But I've got plenty of that fancy root beer your cousin Erik likes and the best iced tea in town, if you're on the wagon for some reason."

"Janie—"

So they were back to *Janie*. She wished she knew him well enough—knew him at *all*—to understand what significance that held. If any.

She stretched her lips in a superbly bright smile. "Jerry's got fresh pecan pie over in the grill, if you're looking for a bite. He's been perfecting it to enter in the Harvest Festival bake-off in a few weeks."

"I don't want any pie."

She shrugged. "Suit yourself. But it's half-off today." Judging by the home Casey had, she was guessing he didn't need to worry about saving a few bucks on a piece of pie, or anything else, for that matter. She looked beyond him and raised her voice. "Axel, you want some of Jerry's pecan pie?"

The tall blond man was racking the balls. "Sounds good to me, Jane. Thanks."

"Coming up." She tossed the towel down by the sink and even though she could have entered the order from her register behind the bar, she headed toward the grill—and away from Casey.

She wanted to dawdle, but she didn't. She was the only one manning the bar at that hour, so leaving it unattended wasn't an option. She served up the thick wedge of pie herself, grabbed a napkin and silverware to go with it and carried it all back into the bar.

Casey hadn't moved.

Ignoring him, she took the pie over to the high-top

next to Axel's pool table and set it there. "Jerry's outdone himself," she told him easily. "Enjoy."

Then, because she couldn't really avoid it, she went back behind the bar and returned to her chores.

"We should talk."

Her shoulders stiffened when Casey spoke. She climbed up on her step stool so she could better reach the shelves with the garland. "Can't imagine why."

"About what happened."

She wished that her bar were crowded to the gills, because he never would think about broaching personal matters if they'd be easily overheard. "We made a point not to talk about that stuff from the get-go." She stretched farther, draping and pinning cobwebs like some sort of decorating maniac. "Don't see any reason for a policy change now."

"Dammit, Janie—"

"Was just habit," she spoke over him. "A bad sexship habit, but nothing to lose sleep over. Not for me, anyway." It was such a blatant lie she was tempted to check whether her nose was growing. And when the phone hanging on the wall next to the register rang, she was pathetically grateful to scramble off the ladder and answer it.

It was Arlo. Either God was punishing her for her sins or sending her a life vest. She honestly wasn't sure which. But either way, she pushed far more enthusiasm than she felt into her greeting. "Arlo! I can't wait for Sunday. I even went out and bought myself a new outfit." She *had* bought a new dress over at Classic Charms. But only because it had been on sale, left over from summer. Wearing it to an outdoor picnic in October would never work.

Mercifully, Casey seemed to give up and returned to the pool table across the room.

She kept her back toward him and pulled in a deep, necessary breath.

Arlo was talking in her ear, saying something sweet about his looking forward to it, too, and guilt congealed inside her. But it wasn't enough to make her do what her conscience demanded: cancel the date.

Not with Casey standing fifty feet away.

Finally, the call ended and she hung up, only to have the thing ring again before she'd even taken away her hand. She picked it up, expecting Arlo had forgotten to relay some detail.

But it wasn't Arlo.

It was her ex-husband, and true surprise swept through her. Since their divorce nearly ten years earlier, their encounters—despite his involvement in her purchase of Colbys—had been few and far between. Not because of acrimony, but simply because he was always busy. He was a died-in-the-wool workaholic. He had been before their divorce and nothing had changed after. The only thing that had was that his work had paid off. He'd become ridiculously successful along the way. And as a way of making it up to her for the failed marriage, he'd given her the means to buy Colbys. "Gage! How are you?"

Casey heard her greeting from across the room and biffed the shot he'd lined up so badly that Axel practically howled with laughter.

He ignored his cousin and tried to listen to Janie's end of the conversation. But she still had her back turned, and though the volume on the jukebox was low at that particular time of day, it was loud enough that he could catch only one word out of every ten.

Whether he could hear or not, though, he could still read the visual cues, including the way she suddenly reached out for the stool she kept behind the bar and sat down. The way she rested her forehead in her hand, nodding occasionally as she listened, the receiver clutched in her fist.

She'd told him, shortly after they'd squabbled their way into bed together, how her ex-husband had enabled her purchase of Colbys. He'd said then, and he'd still say it now, that a financial investment of that magnitude meant there were more ties left between them than she admitted. That there was still unfinished business between her and her ex-husband. She, of course, had contradicted him pretty much the way she contradicted most everything he said.

But there'd been no point in arguing with her about it. As she'd said then, why did it matter to him, anyway? It wasn't as if he had any cause for jealousy. There were no emotional entanglements between her and Casey.

Continuing to gnaw at the issue might have suggested otherwise.

So he'd left it alone.

And now Janie was showing all the signs of shocked devastation over whatever was being said by her ex-husband.

She hung up the phone, and even from across the bar, Casey could see her pallor before she disappeared into the storeroom.

He stuck his cue back on the wall rack and headed after her.

"'Bout damn time," he thought he heard Axel mutter behind him, but he couldn't be sure, because his cousin had a mouthful of pecan pie.

She was in her office, hunched over in her chair, staring blankly at her computer screen. The same one she'd said she was going to replace but obviously had not.

And the second he stepped into view, she stiffened. "Authorized personnel only back here."

He crouched beside her chair, spinning it around so she had to face him. "What's wrong?"

She did her level best to push his hands off the chair arms but was no match for him. After a moment, she gave up and crossed her arms tightly over her chest. "I'm sorry." Her cool tone said she was anything but. "Didn't we establish already that sharing what's upsetting us is *very* clearly out of bounds?"

He frowned. He wasn't likely to forget what had occurred when she'd shown up at his house. He didn't want to verbally regurgitate those events, but he knew she deserved something from him. An apology at the very least. "That was a bad night. I didn't handle it very well."

She looked away, but not quickly enough to hide the sheen in her eyes, and he felt even more like the crumb he was.

"I'm sorry," he said gruffly. "Don't cry."

"Don't flatter yourself." She dashed the back of her hand over her cheek. "I'm upset because my mother-in-law, *former* mother-in-law, had a major stroke last night. She died this morning. She was a really great lady and deserves my tears."

Whereas he didn't. Message received loud and clear.

"I'm sorry," he said again. He'd lost two people— probably three—whom he'd spent the past few years trying to protect. But that wasn't something he could share. He pushed to his feet. "Is there anything I can do?"

Her brows pulled together as she eyed him. "Like what?" Her lips twisted. "You want to go with me to her funeral? You've got an appropriate suit, at least."

His jaw tightened at her sarcasm. "Yeah." The word

was abrupt, coming out before he thought better of it. "I'll go with you."

Her frown smoothed, only because the sarcasm had gone lax with disbelief.

"Unless you'd rather have your new boyfriend with you. *Arlo*," he prompted when she just stared.

"You're serious," she said slowly. "You'd go with me to Althea's funeral. It'll be in Denver."

The back of his neck pricked defensively. "I said so, didn't I?" He pushed his fingers into the front pockets of his jeans. "But I'm sure you'd prefer your sister."

"Already trying to get out of it. Figures."

He managed not to swear. "I'm not trying—"

"Don't sweat it, Casey," she said. "As it happens, my sister is traveling with her husband for the next few weeks. But I'm a big girl. I can get myself to Denver and back all by myself." She swiveled her chair around to face the computer and hit the power button. "You'd just get called into solving some video game emergency anyway."

The computer remained dead silent.

She would try the patience of a saint. And he was definitely no saint. Not even close.

He spun her chair around again. "I *said* I would go with you."

Her expression was mutinous. But her throat worked. And the sheen in her eyes grew until big fat tears, two of them, crept slowly down her cheeks. The coffee-brown of her eyes had turned to wet, glowing amber. "Why?"

He straightened again. Moved away from her before he did something stupid. "Because we're friends." He pushed out the gruff words. "So just…just let me know when it is and I'll be there. Okay?"

She swallowed. Moistened her lips. Then slowly nodded. "Okay."

Chapter Seven

Three days later, Jane was heading up the stairs of a private Cee-Vid jet parked on a runway just outside Weaver she hadn't even known existed.

She was still wondering why she'd agreed to Casey's offer.

It had made no sense at the time he'd made it. Once Gage had finalized the details for the memorial service and she'd relayed them to Casey, it had seemed even less sensible.

Particularly when he'd insisted there was no reason they needed to spend seven or eight hours in a car driving all the way to Denver when he had access to Cee-Vid's transportation, which could make quick work of it.

Yes, she knew the gaming company was successful. There were commercials on television for new releases of their various games. Both children and adults clamored for every system they produced. And though she considered it an odd quirk that the billion-dollar company was headquartered in little Weaver, she chalked it up to the fact that the CEO, Tristan Clay, was loyal to his hometown. Locally, the company employed a few hundred people. She could only guess how many worked at its other locations but figured it had to be hundreds more.

But it still surprised the heck out of her to learn the company had its own jet that evidently flew right out of its own airstrip.

She wasn't looking forward to the trip.

Not with Casey.

Not to say goodbye to a woman who'd been as decent and hardworking as Althea had been.

Her nerves felt knotted as Jane stepped onto the plane. Inside, it resembled someone's professionally decorated living room a lot more than any other passenger plane she'd ever seen.

She looked at Casey behind her. He was ducking his head to clear the top of the doorway as he entered.

She quickly looked away, tightening her grip on the overnighter she was carrying.

The memorial service was later that afternoon. They could have made the trip there and back in one day, except Gage had asked her to stay after the service. The family was having a private dinner at the Denver Ritz-Carlton and even though, technically, she was no longer part of the family, he'd still wanted her there. Her ex-husband had promised to take care of the hotel accommodations, and he'd even included Casey in the invitation when she'd warned Gage she was bringing a "friend."

She'd tried using the dinner as a reason for Casey to change his mind. But he'd been unswerving, telling her to stop arguing when she'd reminded him that family dinners—former or current—weren't part of their world.

So here they were.

She moistened her lips and stepped across plush taupe carpet farther into the plane.

"Give it up, sport. That needs to be stored. Coat, too, if you want." Casey's hand brushed hers as he took the tote from her that she'd insisted on carrying herself while she shrugged out of her knee-length black dress coat. He opened a hidden cupboard and hung everything inside, along with the small battered duffel he'd brought. Then he shut the cupboard with a soft snap and gestured toward the six comfortable-looking chairs. "Take your pick."

Feeling a little as if she'd fallen down the rabbit hole, she took the nearest chair. It was like sinking into a cloud. Even the upholstery felt more like velvet than the leather it was. There was a lap belt to fasten—the only item reminiscent of a regular airplane seat. Otherwise, the chair rocked and swiveled, and she suspected it would recline if she knew how to do it.

He took the seat opposite her and stretched out his long legs. His black shoes were polished and seemed more fitting for a Wall Street banker than the man she knew. He was wearing the same black suit he'd worn the day he'd returned her wallet. But today the shirt was dark with tiny ivory checks—still as far away from psychedelic floral prints as it could get—and the tie was black. He hadn't brought an overcoat.

The door to the cockpit opened and a clean-cut young man in a white shirt and navy slacks appeared. "Good afternoon." He greeted Jane with a professionally polite smile. Then his tone went a shade deferential. "We'll be under way in a few minutes, Mr. Clay."

"Sounds good, Tim."

Unlike Jane, who was watching the young man— Tim—hit a lever that retracted the steps, Casey was watching *her*. It was all she could do not to shift nervously in her chair. Instead, she brushed her palms down the skirt of her plain black dress to smooth it on her thighs and pretended to ignore him.

Once the stairs had disappeared into some magical cavern she couldn't see from her position, Tim secured the outer door and went back through the cockpit door, which he closed behind him.

Even though she knew she and Casey weren't alone on the plane, it suddenly felt as if they were.

She pressed her lips together and crossed her legs.

Casey's hooded gaze seemed to drop to them.

She shifted and crossed them the other way and turned her chair so she could look out the porthole window beside her. Beyond the single runway—which had only one tiny building alongside it, where Casey had parked his truck—there was just open field, gold with dying grass, and wide blue sky overhead.

"Never figured you for a nervous flier."

It wasn't the flying that made her nervous. It was him. And she wasn't about to admit it. "When I'm on a plane that looks bigger than a toy, I'm not."

She wasn't looking at him, but she felt his amusement at that.

"So tell me about Althea."

She chewed the inside of her lip. The plane was already moving, engines roaring as they picked up speed down the paved strip. She guessed that was one advantage of having a private airstrip: not having to wait in lines for other planes to take off. "She was Gage's mother." She stated the obvious. She realized she was holding her breath when the plane whooshed, leaving the ground. Then she sighed as the landscape below rapidly fell away from the plane. She shifted again in the chair, nudging the carpet with the toe of her black pump to turn the chair toward him once more.

"Is his dad still alive?"

"No. Gage never knew him. He died before Gage was even a year old. Althea raised him and his brother, Noah, on her own."

"Older?"

"Younger. They had different fathers." She didn't know how to describe Noah, exactly, so she didn't try. He'd barely been a teenager when she and Gage had divorced. And even at just thirteen, he'd been a handful. "Althea never married either one. She was an extremely independent woman."

"And another example of why *you* want to be married before you have a kid?"

"Althea wasn't like my mom. They might have both chosen their paths, but that's their only similarity." She lifted her shoulder. "My mom got pregnant when she was seventeen. She kicked out my father when I was seven." And Jane had a very clear memory of that dreadful time. The screaming. The crying. "Julia was five."

"You admired Althea. But not your mom."

She frowned. "I never said that."

"You didn't have to, sport. I can hear it in your voice every time you talk about her. You told me a few years ago that she'd died before you moved to Weaver. But why'd she kick him out?"

"No idea."

"You didn't ask?"

"Of course I asked! She *had* no good reason. None she offered. And now she's gone, so there's no point wondering anymore anyway!"

He rested his head against the back of his chair. His

long fingers were loosely linked across the flat plane of his stomach. He looked completely relaxed and at ease.

But his gray eyes were watchful. And they made her feel anything but at ease.

"What happened after your dad left? You and Julia spend any time with him?"

"Never saw him again. Last I heard, he was in California with a whole new legitimate family. Evidently, he wasn't against marriage. Just against marriage to my mother."

He frowned a little. "If you have siblings out there in the world, aren't you curious about them?"

"Would you be?"

He let that pass, revealing nothing, which was typical for him. "And you blamed your mom for it all."

She exhaled. "Hayley Templeton's the one qualified to be a therapist. Not you."

"Some things don't need fancy schooling to figure out."

She didn't have a response for that. Not a polite one, anyway, and manners at least dictated that she try not to argue with him outright while on a private plane ride *he* had arranged.

"So did you get permission to use the plane because Tristan Clay's your uncle, or because you're oh-so-important to the company he owns?"

His lips twitched. "Pretty obvious change of subject there, Janie." He glanced out the window beside him as the plane leveled off, then unfastened his safety belt and stood. He shrugged out of his suit coat and tossed it over the back of the vacant chair next to him.

"That's going to wrinkle."

"So?"

"So you should hang it up."

"It's fine."

She caught herself from letting out a huff. "Fine. You're a grown man. If you want to be wrinkled, that's your business."

"You just can't stand it when someone doesn't do what you think they should do."

She ignored that. "So? Which is it? I mean, do I need to send a thank-you note to your uncle?"

"Do you practice being annoying, or were you born with the gift?" He pulled his tie loose a few inches and freed the collar button. Then he opened another cupboard door much like the one hiding the storage compartment where he'd stowed their bags. But this one hid a refrigerator. He pulled out two bottles of water and tossed her one, then returned to his seat, hitching one ankle over his knee.

Manners be damned. "Back atcha, *sport*." She twisted open the plastic cap and drank. "As it happens, nobody else seems to find me particularly annoying. So I guess it is just you who brings out the best in me."

"What'd you tell Arlo?"

She pressed her tongue against the back of her teeth, gathering her scattered wits. "Nothing to tell," she said. "I'm just going home to Denver for a memorial service."

"With another man."

She was glad for the water. It gave her hands something to do and combatted her dry mouth. "With another *friend*." She took a few more sips, then waved the bottle around, taking in the luxurious interior. "That's why we're here, isn't it?"

His lips looked a little thin, but he gave a nod, acknowledging the point. "So what else is there about Althea?"

Frustration gurgled inside her. "She, um, she worked for a guy named Julian Locke."

"Of Locke Technologies?"

She didn't know why she was surprised he'd have heard of the Colorado-based company. "Yeah. She was his assistant for twenty-five years. Gage was working there when we met in college. I was a freshman. He was a senior." The details didn't seem to particularly interest him and she felt foolish for having offered them. She sipped the water and turned again to look out the window. The flight would only take a little while longer than a commercial one. And since they hadn't needed to drive to Gillette first to catch a flight, it would come out even in the end. "This *is* a pretty nice airplane."

"I'll tell my uncle you approve."

Despite herself, she felt a smile tug at her lips.

They landed about an hour later. Jane's ex-husband had sent a car that took them straight to the church where the service was being held. They were a little early, but not enough to stop off at their hotel and get checked in.

Early or not, Jane's ex-husband was already there. Even though Casey had never met Gage Stanton, he knew plenty about the other man, though not from Jane. He didn't even feel guilty about poking his cyber nose into his business.

What Casey didn't know, though, was what kind of ties still existed between Jane and him.

That they *did* exist was obvious as hell when the tall dark-haired man wrapped his arms around Jane, lifting her right off her black high heels as he hugged her tightly and kissed her square on the lips.

It was all Casey could do not to rip her away from the man.

Finally, Gage set her down and looked over her head at Casey.

Jane, still nestled against her ex-husband's side, turned her gaze back on Casey, too. He saw tears in her eyes again. She licked her lips and tucked her hair behind her ears. It was one of the few times Casey had ever seen her leave it down. Outside of bed, that was.

She waved her hand toward him. "Gage. This is Casey Clay."

No other explanation. Maybe she'd already given one. How the hell was Casey supposed to know?

"Casey." Gage held out his hand. "Good to meet you."

Casey wasn't so sure. He shook Gage's hand, though, mentally taking the other man's measure, knowing his was being taken in return. Gage was just as tall as Casey. A little heavier. A few years older. His grip was firm. Casey had no reason to dislike him, except for his connection to Jane.

And the proprietary arm the guy still had around her shoulder.

"My condolences," he offered.

Jane's gaze skipped from Casey's back to Gage's. "I'm just going to freshen up, and then Casey and I should probably get inside. There'll be other people you'll need to greet. Noah—"

Gage's lips tightened. "He won't be here."

Jane squeezed his arm. She didn't look surprised. "I'm sorry," she murmured. Then, flicking another glance at Casey—which had a warning in it as if she were afraid he'd misbehave or something—she hurried down the hall off the church entrance where they were standing.

She was obviously familiar with the church's layout. She knew where she was heading.

He wondered if she and Gage had been married at the

church, too. Maybe it was where all family events were observed. The same way the Weaver Community Church saw most of the Clay family weddings and burials.

"You and Jane been friends long?"

Casey met the other man's eyes. "Since she bought Colbys." He remembered the first time he'd met her. He'd thought she was beautiful. And a snob. They'd gotten along like oil and water. Calling themselves friends for that duration was an exaggeration. One he didn't feel a speck of conscience over, even if they were in a church.

He'd learned she was no snob. But it seemed the oil-and-water thing still applied as often as not.

Unless they were in bed together.

He brushed aside the thought.

"The bar and grill's become more successful than it ever was before you bought it for her," he added. The manner in which she'd acquired his favorite hangout shouldn't have bugged Casey. But it did.

"She tried paying me back." Gage was unsmiling. "But I figured she deserved the place after putting up with me for the two years we were married. Is it serious between you two?"

He guessed it was up to the other man whether or not he wanted to get into that on the doorstep of his mother's memorial service. But Casey figured Gage had had nearly ten years since their divorce to get Jane back if he'd wanted.

And oil could mix with water for a while if it was shaken hard enough.

"Serious enough." He glanced down the hallway she'd taken and saw no sign of her yet. "She wants a baby."

The other man's eyebrows shot up. "You're kidding me."

Casey had grown up going to Sunday school. He still

stuck his head into church on Christmas and Easter and whenever his mom gave him that look that said he'd been absent for too long. So he believed in God, even though he didn't generally feel the call to put his hind end in a pew every Sunday. But since the roof of this particular church hadn't crashed down on him yet, he took another chance and shook his head. "No joke. Janie wants a baby."

"Didn't think I'd ever see that day." Gage scrubbed his hand over his cheek, then stuck it out toward Casey again. Casey must have passed muster with the other man, because there was only a glint of surprise left in his eyes. "Well, good luck to you, then," Gage said. "Jane's one of a kind." He shook Casey's hand, then lifted it to acknowledge another person entering the church behind them and excused himself.

Jane returned a few minutes later. She'd removed her coat and rubbed some shiny stuff on her lips, making the pink a little pinker, and brushed out her hair. He wasn't used to seeing her wear high heels, and in the narrow black dress that clung to her figure, she seemed both familiar to him and unfamiliar.

There wasn't a part of her body that he hadn't explored.

He knew everything except the things that ticked inside her brain.

And her heart.

But he'd been getting enough glimpses to know there was no possible way things between them could go back to the way they were before. And, given her plans, going forward was just as impossible.

"Everything all right?" she murmured when she rejoined him. She glanced at Gage, who was greeting another older couple who'd just arrived. There was a steady stream of people now coming into the church.

Gage and Casey hadn't come to blows. He figured that was something. "Fine." He closed his hand over her elbow, feeling the slight jerk of surprise she gave, and steered her through the double doors that closed off the sanctuary from the entry where they were all gathering.

She slid into one of the pews near the back, well away from the clusters of people who were already seated, and draped her coat over the pew beside her, then unfolded the program that an usher handed them. She kept running her thumb nervously along the edge of the thick parchment paper. "I'm glad it's a memorial and not a funeral," she whispered. "Althea would have hated a funeral. She told me once she never wanted to be in a box on display."

Casey pushed away the image of Jonathan's casket and curled his program into a cone. He leaned his head closer to her. "What's the deal with Noah?"

She let out a faint sound. "He was a selfish, entitled brat when he was thirteen," she whispered. "I'm guessing nothing's changed. I feel sorry for Gage, though. He's sixteen years older than Noah. I think Althea always expected him to be more father figure to him than brother."

"Is that all you feel for Gage?"

Her eyes lifted. Her lips firmed, and he thought she wouldn't answer.

"He's a better *ex* than he was a husband," she finally said. Then she shushed Casey and tugged a hymnal from the rack in front of them. She pushed it into his hand. "I assume you know what that's for."

He gave her a look and flipped the book open to the first hymn listed in the program.

A long ninety minutes later, Casey's butt was numb from the wooden pew, and Janie was sniffling into the white handkerchief he'd offered her when she'd started rooting around in her tiny purse and had come up with only one square of tissue.

But the service was over and she seemed glad to leave just as immediately as he was.

The same car they'd arrived in was waiting, and they took it to the hotel. Unfortunately, the hotel had only one room reserved for them.

And it was sold out otherwise.

Janie's cheeks were flushed, but without argument, she grabbed the key card the clerk gave them and headed toward the elevator bank, leaving Casey to wonder if she'd known there would be only one room. If she'd warned Gage she was bringing a "friend."

If she'd given the matter any thought at all.

He yanked at his tie, loosening it again.

As many times as they'd slept together, they'd never *slept* together.

Casey looked at the reception clerk. "Dude. Cut me some slack here." He pulled out his wallet and discreetly set his credit card on the desk. Beneath it were several folded bills. Working for Hollins-Winword, he'd stayed in hundreds of hotels around the world. He knew the way this all worked. "There's *always* a room left."

The clerk's gaze darted left. Then right. "It's a suite, sir."

"I don't care what it is," he assured him.

The clerk ran the credit card and programmed another key card that he slid into a thick paper sleeve. He wrote the number on it. "Two floors down from your friend." To the hotel's credit, the guy didn't take the cash. Casey took it, and the key card, and picked up his duffel, then reached across and shook the guy's hand. "Thanks."

"My pleasure, sir."

Tip—he preferred that term over *bribe*—duly transferred unseen into the guy's palm, Casey followed Jane to the elevators where she was still waiting.

"Don't worry." He tapped the key card against her chin. "Your virtue is safe from me."

The elevator doors chimed softly and slid open.

"It's not my virtue I'm worried about," she murmured, and entered the empty car ahead of him. She punched the button for the top floor and for his floor as well before he could, then moved to the rear corner of the car, leaning her head back with a sigh. She slid her right foot out of its shoe. She was wearing sheer black nylons, and watching her wiggle her narrow ankle around was oddly entrancing.

They'd just been to a memorial service.

And she *should* have been worrying about her virtue. Because all men were dogs, and he was no better.

He was glad when she slid her foot back into her shoe.

The light on the panel steadily worked its way from button to button. Third floor. Fourth. "What is it that you *do* worry about?"

"Dying alone." She sighed the words immediately, as if they'd already been on her tongue. Circling in her thoughts. She straightened, giving him a thin smile he guessed was meant to discount the answer.

"Is that why you want a husband?" He wasn't going to touch the baby topic with a ten-foot pole. "You think that'll keep you from being lonely?"

She closed her eyes. Shook her head. "Casey, it was… nice…of you to come with me." She made a sound. "To bring me here, even." She opened her eyes again but didn't look at him. "But I'm not up to a round of verbal sparring with you. And I'm not lonely."

"Never?"

She exhaled. She lifted her palms. "What do you want

me to say?" The elevator hummed to a smooth stop and the doors slid open to the accompaniment of a soft musical chime. She looked at the display, needlessly. "This is your floor." She hitched the long strap of her tote higher over her shoulder. "Gage has dinner set up in a private dining room downstairs at six. He specifically told me to bring you, but I'll just meet you there, okay?"

She looked tired. But even with the smudges beneath her eyes, she was still prettier than a new spring foal on his grandfather's ranch.

Prettier. And, for the first time since he'd known her, just as delicate.

"Okay."

Chapter Eight

Knowing her ex-husband the way she did, once Jane found her way later that evening to the room where the dinner was being held, she wasn't surprised at the lavish display he'd arranged in his mother's memory.

She'd changed from the black dress into a dark purple one—less funereal but still modestly sober as long as she kept the surplice front tugged above her cleavage—but she hadn't brought another pair of dress heels, so she'd pushed her protesting toes back into the black pumps after her failed attempt at having a nap. She'd started to tie up her hair but hadn't.

Althea had always liked her with her hair down. Just as purple had always been her mother-in-law's favorite color.

Neither choice made up for not having spoken with the woman except through the exchange of Christmas and birthday letters for the past few years, but it made Jane feel a little better.

There were already a dozen people milling around the room when she arrived. They all had cocktails in hand and gave off the impression that the dinner was more of a social event than what it really was. Which was also a detail that would have suited Althea immensely.

Gage was easy to spot. He was deep in conversation with Quigley Decker, the vice president of Stanton Development, and didn't notice her at all.

Aside from him and Quig, she didn't recognize anyone. Sighing a little, she wished she'd told Gage that she wouldn't be staying after the memorial service. Had she done so, she and Casey would already be back home again.

As if her thoughts had conjured him, he appeared, stopping next to her where she was hovering just inside the doorway of the private room. "I've seen you wear more dresses in one single day than in all the time I've known you. You clean up real good, sport."

She managed a small smile.

He hadn't changed anything. From the tie knotted perfectly at his neck to his gleaming wing-tip shoes, he looked unfamiliarly urbane.

He tilted his head toward her a little and dropped his voice. "If I hadn't seen you naked as many times as I have, I might never have known you had legs."

Her face heated. Annoyed, she shot him a look.

He gave a satisfied smile. "There you are." He cupped her elbow in his warm palm. "Can't stand seeing that waifish look on your face. Makes me feel all protective-like, and I know you'd be the first to deny you needed any protecting from anyone."

"At least that's something you got right." Her arm was tingling beneath his touch, but he didn't let go as she aimed for the cocktail bar set up in the corner of the room.

Would Casey ever protect her if she needed it?

She mentally brushed away the futile thought as if it were an irritating gnat. But like all good irritating gnats, it kept coming back, hovering around, dodging all of her efforts to dispose of it.

She ordered a white wine and turned, glass in hand, to survey the room while the tuxedoed bartender poured Casey's red.

In all the years he'd been patronizing Colbys, she'd never once served him wine. White, red or otherwise. He was a beer man through and through, with only the occasional whiskey thrown in on special occasions.

The only time he'd had wine of any sort was when he'd brought that one bottle to her place.

"I'm surprised you didn't order a beer." There were several bottles of craft beer, labels turned out, on the portable bar's tasteful display.

He tipped the rim of his glass against hers and the crystal clinked softly. "Guess there are things about me you don't know either." He settled his hand against the small of her back as if it were the most natural thing in the world. "You want to sit or mingle?"

The warmth from his fingers was burning through her dress. A few people had found spots along the long rectangular table already, so they wouldn't be the first. "Sit." The word emerged more abruptly than she intended. Spurred, no doubt, by self-preservation.

If she were sitting, he couldn't very well keep his hand on her back.

She quickly led the way around the table, choosing two seats at the far end. Casey was left-handed. He'd want to be on the outside, where he'd have more room.

Before he could, she pulled out her own chair and then sank down on it with embarrassing haste.

"My feet are killing me." She muttered the excuse when he slid a look her way. To prove it, beneath the veil of the white linen tablecloth that reached all the way to the floor, she slipped her bare feet out of the torturous pumps. She'd ditched the black nylons along with the black dress. Probably a mistake in hindsight; the hosiery would have been a welcome buffer between her feet and the beastly toe-pinching leather.

She much preferred her boots or tennis shoes, or nothing at all.

He pulled out his chair and sat down, then stretched his arm across the back of her chair.

He might have just been making himself comfortable.

Or deliberately spreading on a fresh layer of torment.

With Casey, it was difficult to tell.

He angled his head toward hers. "You don't know anyone here at all, other than your ex-husband." It wasn't a question.

She shook her head. "No. Oh, well, I know Quig. Quigley Decker. He's Gage's right hand." She shifted in her chair, the better to put some space between Casey's distracting fingers and her shoulder. "How did you know?"

His fingers tapped the back of her neck, then returned to grazing her shoulder. "Come on, sport. You haven't said so much as a hello to anyone. If these were people you used to be related to, you'd be at least offering a hello-how-are-you even if you loathed them."

She gave up and sat back comfortably in her seat, because his hand seemed determined to stay put no matter what she did. "Althea didn't have a lot of family. I think that older couple over there in the corner might have worked at Locke with her—they look vaguely familiar.

But I'm guessing the rest here work with Gage." She took a quick drink of her wine when she felt him twirl his finger in her hair.

Was he doing it deliberately? Or was it just an automatic reflex designed to disturb her?

"Who divorced whom?"

"What?" She looked at him.

He was idly rubbing the thumb of his left hand along the rim of his glass. "Did you leave him or did he leave you?"

She shook her head a little. "I can't believe you're asking me that here."

He glanced around. The chairs next to and across from them were still empty. Gage was still standing across the room, talking to Quig. Casey's point was clear—nobody was paying them any attention at all. They might have been alone together. "Something else you'd like to talk about?" he asked mildly. "The weather, maybe? You think we'll have an early or late snow?"

She exhaled. "I'm the one who filed," she finally said. "But Gage knew it was coming." She gestured subtly with her wineglass toward her ex-husband. "He spent more time working than he did with me. Neither one of us was even brokenhearted. If that doesn't prove we should have never gotten married in the first place, I don't know what would." The admission had come much too easily and she took a hasty sip of wine. "At least you've been smart enough not to make the same mistake."

His lips twisted a little. "You'd think." His gray gaze slid over her. "But I was engaged. Once upon a time."

Her jaw loosened. She stared. The puzzle pieces where he was concerned shifted around into a whole new, equally indecipherable pattern. "When?" Certainly not in the five years she'd lived in Weaver. She'd have heard about it.

"College."

He wore a wry expression that struck her as too practiced and she angled her legs toward him, studying him more closely. His eyes were annoyingly unreadable. "What happened?"

"Turns out we wanted different things." He sipped his wine, then set his glass back on the linen. The corner of his lips jerked slightly. "She changed her mind."

"Hmm." Jane realized she was studying the shape of those mobile lips. Somehow or other, her knees were pressed against his beneath the tablecloth. She took a quick gulp of wine. "Probably got tired of being left dangling while you went to play with your Cee-Vid games."

Something came and went in his eyes. The quirk at the corner of his lips deepened. "Probably." The one word dripped with sarcasm.

But she didn't have a chance to pursue it, because just then Gage moved over to the head of the table and lifted his glass. "To my mother," he said. "A woman ahead of her time." His voice went a little gruff. "She's gone too soon, but she'd have my head if she thought any of us were crying in our soup. So. Althea Stanton." He cleared his throat. "One hell of a grand old broad. You'll be missed."

Jane's eyes flooded, but she couldn't help smiling. Because the woman she'd known—the woman who'd actually applauded Jane's decision to divorce her workaholic, inattentive son—had been exactly what Gage described.

She lifted her glass and drank to her memory.

And was glad that Casey's palm had curled warmly around her shoulder.

After that, the waiters arrived, delivering plates of

food so beautifully prepared they seemed more like works of art than something to be consumed. And though Jane hadn't expected to feel hungry, she realized she was.

Along with the food, though, came more wine, which one of the servers kept pouring into her glass.

By the time crème brûlée was served—Althea's favorite, just as the endive-and-frisée salad and the fancily presented lamb chops had been—Jane could hardly see straight.

Casey recognized it, too. It wasn't hard, given the way she was slumping farther and farther down in her chair as she reminisced about her former mother-in-law.

"Shewasagreat, great lady." Jane slurred slightly. She picked up her wineglass to emphasize her words, trying to enunciate and failing ridiculously. "When I'm gone, I'd like to think somebody says that about me."

"I'm sure they will." He slid the glass out of her lax fingers. Most everyone was beginning to depart, except for her ex-husband and a few others. They were talking about the latest resort Stanton Development was planning.

"Wha—?" She frowned at Casey, belatedly noticing what he'd done. She planted her index finger in the center of his chest. "I wasn't finished with my wine."

"Trust me, sport. You're finished." He wrapped his hand around hers and kissed her knuckles. "You'll thank me in the morning."

Her lips parted. She blinked at him.

Realizing what he'd done, he squeezed her fingers and managed a goading grin. "Who knew the bartender couldn't hold her drink?"

She pressed her lips together in a pout she'd regret if she ever remembered it. "I can, too."

He pulled her to her feet. Her bare feet, since she'd

discarded her shoes somewhere beneath the floor-length tablecloth.

"Whoops." She wiggled her toes. "Missing somethin'." She started to bend down and nearly lost her balance, butting her head accidentally into his ribs. "Whoa there, baby."

"That's my line." He steadied her. "I'll get them." Keeping one hand on her slender hip, he knelt down to fish out the shoes. They were shiny black leather with pointy toes, lethal heels and tiny little leather bows. "Lift."

She clamped her hand over her mouth, covering her giggle as she "helpfully" tried to push her toes into the shoe.

He smiled despite himself and caught her ankle, holding it still so he could get her shoe in place.

"Ouch." She made a face when he was finally successful. "I *hate* high heels." She stuck her other foot out, wriggling it around. Her toenails were painted a bright pink. "I'm sure they were created by some *man*."

He corralled that foot, too. "Why's that?"

"Jus' 'cause women's butts look better when they're wearing high heels," she muttered.

He choked back a laugh. The shoes were sexy as hell. But her butt needed no assistance in the looking-perfect department. "Sweetheart, next time you'd better stop after two glasses." He straightened and cautiously took his hand away from her hip.

"You never call me sweetheart." She turned toward the door, spotted Gage and aimed—listing a little sideways—toward him. The other man caught her up for a hug and eyed Casey over her head as if he were to blame for the fact that she was obviously tipsy.

He'd take the blame. Particularly if it kept Gage from thinking he ought to see Janie to her room personally.

He tugged her away from Gage and steered her out of the private dining room, down the corridor to the elevators. The doors slid open as soon as he pushed the call button, and he nudged her inside and pushed the top-floor button.

The car started its ascent and she took a steadying step, bumping into him. "Stupid shoes," she muttered.

He scrubbed his hand down his face to keep from laughing. "Why'd you wear them if you hate them so much?"

"'Cause that's what you do when you wear a nice dress," she said as if the reasoning were obvious. "If I wore flats, my ankles would look like tree stumps."

It was a lost cause. Laughter barked out of him. "Trust me, Janie. Your ankles will *never* look like tree stumps."

She smiled, then rubbed her eyes. "Contacts're killin' me."

"You can take them out as soon as we get you into your room," he assured her. Which led him to the next issue. She wasn't carrying a purse. "Where's your room key?"

She inhaled deeply, then reached into the purple fabric that crisscrossed over her breasts in a V that had distracted him all evening. "Ta-daa." She pulled the key card out just as the elevator chimed.

He took the card from her and steered her out of the elevator. The card was warm from having been tucked into her bra all evening. And when they reached her room, it didn't work.

He tried again.

"I bet I demag—" she sighed and slid down onto her butt with her back against the wall "—netized it."

Being pressed against her breasts all night would have had the opposite effect on him.

"Happens all the time." She lifted her hands, palms upward, to display her unadorned wrists. "Don't have good luck with watches either."

Trying not to look at her smooth legs, bared almost all the way up her thighs thanks to the way her dress had hiked up as she slid down the wall, he tried the card a last time with the same results. Which was to say no results at all.

"Come on." He wrapped his hands around hers to pull her to her feet again. "We'll have to go down and get it reprogrammed."

She resisted his tug. "Can't you go?"

"I could. But I'd have no respect for the security in this place if they gave *me* a key to *your* room." He pulled. "Come on, sport."

Grumbling, she made it to her feet and the hem of her dress slid back down toward her knees. "I'm never gonna wear high heels again."

"Not even with the dress you got for your date with Arlo?"

She exhaled and leaned into him as they retraced their steps to the elevator. "Arlo. He's a nice man." She patted his shoulder. "Not like you."

He snorted. "Thanks."

"I didn't mean you're not *nice*." She poked the call button with exaggerated care. "You came with me for Althea." She tucked her hair behind her ear and peered up at him. "Why'd you do that, Casey? You can't be running to Cee-Vid's rescue when you're here with me in Colorado."

God help him. "Because you were upset. And I didn't want you to be alone."

The elevator doors slid open. "That's why I kissed you," she said. "That, uh, that other night."

As if he didn't remember, exactly and with excruciating detail, the night in question.

He stopped the doors from closing on them before they even had a chance to get on the elevator. "In you go."

She obediently stepped inside with only a slight totter. "'Cause you were upset. I didn't know how else to help."

"You're gonna croak when you think about this conversation tomorrow morning."

"Prob'ly." She propped herself up in the back corner of the elevator. "You stopped 'cause you didn't wan' me to get pregnant."

"What?"

The elevator lurched slightly as it halted on his floor and opened for a waiting couple.

Casey waited until they'd boarded, then yanked Jane off the car before the doors closed again.

"What're you doing?"

He latched his hand around her wrist and pulled her down the hall. *His* key card worked just fine, and he nudged her into his suite.

Her jaw dropped a little as she moved farther into the suite, taking in the luxurious surroundings. "And I thought my room was nice."

He shut the door and dropped the key card on the foyer table and followed her. "I didn't stop that night because I was afraid you'd get pregnant."

She twisted her hair off her neck and held it on top of her head as she worked her way around the living area with its shining glass coffee table, couch and chairs, toward the expansive window overlooking the city lights below and the Rockies beyond. It was a spectacular view.

But it was the back of her slender neck that drew his eyes. He knew it was smooth. Soft. Warm.

And whenever he kissed her there, she shivered.

"You didn't need to worry," she said as if he'd never spoken. "I was still on the pill."

Was.

"So things are moving that fast with good ol' Arlo? You're no longer taking your birth control now that you're seeing him?" His hands curled into fists, hating the thought and knowing he didn't have a hell of a lot of real estate on which to stand.

She didn't answer that. "What's worse? A child in general, or havin' one with me?"

"I *said* that wasn't the reason."

She turned to face him, dropping her twisted hair so that it unfurled past her shoulders and over her breasts into a messy golden curtain of loose curls. "Then what *was*?" Her voice rose. "You treated me like…like a—"

"Dammit, Jane." He cut her off, not wanting to hear her say it. "I was trying to do the right thing!" His tie was strangling him and he yanked it off and balled it in his fist. "I just found out two people I was responsible for were dead and I—"

Her eyes rounded.

He cursed a blue streak, throwing the tie across the room.

"Cee-Vid people? From *Weaver*? Why didn't I hear anything about—?"

"Not from Weaver." He shoved his hands through his hair. He hadn't had anywhere near enough to drink to blame his lapse on it.

"They worked at another location? Was there an accident or—?"

"Yeah. There was an accident. And I don't want to talk

about it now any more than I did that night you came to my house. Are you sleeping with Arlo or not?"

Her lips rounded into a silent *O*. "That's not really any of your business, is it?" she said after a tight moment.

The effects from the wine she'd consumed were obviously waning.

Rapidly.

"It is when you throw yourself at me."

Her eyebrows shot up. "*Throw* myself at you?" She reached out and shoved his chest with both hands. "Get out of my way." He circled her wrists with his hands, easily stopping her attempts, even when she went from shoving to trying to pull away. "Let me go!"

"You don't get to call all the shots all the time, Janie." He squeezed her wrists for emphasis. "You don't come into my house, kissing *me* when you're making dates with someone else."

"I was trying to comfort you!" She yanked, to no avail. "How's that any different than you bringing me here for Althea's service?"

"You've still got your panties on, for one thing."

He regretted the words as soon as he said them.

Her face went red.

Then white.

When she yanked away this time, he let her go.

"I don't know who you are," she said in a hoarse voice, then turned and walked out of the suite, closing the door quietly behind her.

Chapter Nine

Jane rode the Cee-Vid plane back to Weaver alone.

After the debacle with Casey the night before, she'd been glad that morning when she'd found the note he'd slid beneath her hotel room door.

"Take the jet," he'd scrawled on the sheet of hotel stationery in black ink. "I'm sorry."

She'd crumpled the note in her fist and tossed it in the pretty little trash can in the hotel bathroom.

Only to retrieve it an hour later, smooth it out and read it again.

As if the five words would have changed any while she'd showered and pretended it was getting shampoo in her eyes that made them water so.

"We'll be landing in about ten minutes, Ms. Cohen." Tim from the day before had been replaced by Steven, who was equally spit-shined, dressed identically and had obviously been made aware that Jane was traveling alone for the return route to Weaver. He was polite and friendly, offering her choice of water or coffee and serving a platter of fresh fruit.

"Thanks, Steven." She pinched her fingers along the folded edge of the note she was holding and watched him take away the untouched fruit plate. A moment later, he was back behind the cockpit door.

She unfolded the note. The words were the same. The wrinkles from crumpling it earlier were still evident.

She didn't know how Casey was getting back to Weaver.

She told herself she didn't care.

She folded the note again, turned her chair and stared blindly out the window.

Ten minutes later, they were on the ground.

She'd thought she'd need to call someone to pick her up, since Casey had insisted on collecting her from her condo the day before. But when they landed and Steven appeared again to open the outer door and let down the stairs, he handed her a set of keys. "Mr. Clay said to use his truck."

She automatically closed her fingers around the keys.

She had no desire to drive Casey's truck home.

It would mean he'd have to retrieve it from her at some point.

"He'll send someone to get it later today," Steven added.

Which solved that dilemma.

So why did knowing that Casey had covered every detail make her feel so empty inside?

"Thanks, Steven." She hitched the tote bag strap over her shoulder and stepped out of the plane.

The weather was a little warmer than it had been in Denver, which had been overcast when the plane had taken off. Here the sky was clear. The sun promised a perfect autumn day.

Too bad she was in no mood to appreciate it.

She descended the steps, went over to Casey's truck parked next to the little building and drove to Colbys.

It was Friday. She had work to do.

Casey could pick up his truck from there.

She didn't want there to be any reason left for him to come to her condo.

It wasn't yet noon. The grill at Colbys was already open, though Ruby's just down the street had a lock on most of the breakfast business downtown. The bar side was dark. She flipped on the lights and left Casey's keys sitting on the end of the bar.

She could have left them inside his truck. Lots of people did that in Weaver. She was guilty of doing it herself. But she had no idea when he was going to have it picked up or where, and if his disreputable truck was going to be stolen, it wouldn't be on her watch.

The money from the bar and grill's take the night before was in the safe. She paged through the receipts, then took the cash and walked down the street to the bank.

"Hey, Jane." Alberta, the middle-aged teller who'd worked at the bank since Jane had moved to Weaver, was at her usual spot behind the teller's cage when Jane handed over the deposit. "Sorry to hear about your former mother-in-law."

She swallowed her surprise. She should have known her personal business would get around town quickly when she'd made no effort to hide it. "Thank you."

"Hear you and Casey Clay are an item now," Alberta went on, smiling slyly. "He's a fine catch. All of those Clay boys are."

Jane's face felt frozen. "We're just friends," she said

dismissively. Not even that. Not after the things they'd said to one another the night before.

"That's what they all say," Alberta assured her. Her eyes twinkled as she ran Jane's cash through the counting machine. "Morning, Dori," she greeted the next customer who'd entered the bank behind Jane. "How's Howard doing today?"

The older heavyset woman with red sausage curls joined Jane at the counter in front of the other window, which was tended by a girl Jane didn't know. "Ornery as ever. Spraining his ankle thinking he's still young enough to play football with his grandkids just makes him more so." She looked at the teller in front of her. "You're new," she greeted. "I want to cash this check. Give me only fives. And crisp new ones, too."

Jane hid a smile. She knew the five-dollar bills were for Dori's grandkids, who did chores for her every weekend. She also knew that Howard was the widower who lived next door to Dori and, rumor had it, figured they ought to be living together under the same roof but wasn't willing to marry her to bring that about. The quasi couple ate in the grill often but rarely came across to the bar.

The counting machine had finished and Alberta handed Jane her deposit receipt. "I was beginning to wonder if Casey would be all work and no play," she said without missing a stroke. "It's never good when a young man like that ignores romance for too long."

Jane barely kept from cringing. "We're not a couple."

"Sure." Alberta was obviously unconvinced. "Same as Dori there and Howard aren't a couple. Everyone's talking about how Casey stood by, comfortin' you in your time of need. Going to Montana with you 'n' all."

"Colorado," Jane corrected her. Hyperactive or not, Weaver's grapevine was obviously prone to inaccuracies.

Alberta waved off the detail as unimportant. "Point is, sweetie, he went. Men don't do that for a girl they're just—" she sketched a pair of air quotes "'—friends' with." She reached into her drawer and pulled out a flyer that she handed to Jane. "Got a shredder truck coming over next week from Braden, if you need any personal stuff shredded. Bank's sponsoring up to four boxes a person for free. You mind putting that flyer up at Colbys?"

"Happy to." She was desperately glad for the change of topic. "If you give me another one, I'll be able to put one up by both entrances."

Alberta beamed and handed over the second flyer. "You tell that nice boy to behave, now, you hear?"

Jane managed a weak smile and left the bank with indecent haste.

Back at Colbys, she taped up the flyers in the window by the grill entrance and on the back of the door of the bar. Both spots already held a collection of other community announcements. She automatically checked to make sure none of them were out of date, then went back into her office.

Concentrating on her day-to-day tasks wasn't enough to keep Casey from slipping into her thoughts, though. Particularly when she tried to turn on her computer and it refused to cooperate, even after she'd thumped the side of it a few times.

"Great."

Casey could get it running again. He was magic when it came to that sort of stuff.

But she was *not* going to call him to save the day.

There were no computer stores in Weaver. The hardware store sold some electronics, though nothing like what she would probably need. She'd inherited the computer system when she'd bought Colbys and hadn't seen a reason to change it. She could check Shop-World, she supposed. The place seemed to carry everything. But she'd feel better dealing with a place that specialized in computers over a discount superstore that didn't.

She propped her elbows on her desk and kneaded her forehead with her fingertips. "Stupid, stupid, stupid."

"Now, don't say that."

Startled, she looked up. But it wasn't Casey invading her office space; it was Arlo. Her lips parted. "Hi."

He smiled and leaned his shoulder against the doorjamb. "Hope you don't mind me dropping by."

"No," she said faintly. She hadn't gotten hold of him to cancel their Sunday date. Shamefully, she hadn't given him much thought at all after Casey had thrown her for a loop offering to accompany her to Denver. "In fact, I'm glad you did. I—"

"I'm glad, too." His smile widened. "I just got back from Cheyenne. You were the first person I wanted to see."

Her throat tightened. If she were any sort of decent person at all, she should have known that he'd been out of town. But the news was a complete surprise. "That's… that's sweet, Arlo. But—"

"Thought maybe I could talk you into lunch before you get too busy here. I hear Jerry makes a mean grilled cheese sandwich."

Tears suddenly burned her eyes.

He frowned, looking concerned. "What's wrong?"

She shook her head, feeling mortified. "My computer won't work," she said thickly, which just made her feel mortified *and* guilty.

He tsked. "You're upset about your mother-in-law in Montana dying."

"Colorado." She let out a choking laugh that was closer to a sob. "Arlo, you're way, *way* too good for me."

He angled his head. "Why don't you let me be the judge of that?"

He was tall. Not as tall as Casey, but then, few people were. He had light brown hair and blue eyes. Kind blue eyes. Open blue eyes.

There were no secrets hiding behind them.

She chewed the inside of her lip and willed back the tears. "I haven't been honest with you."

His eyebrows lifted. "About what?"

About what, indeed?

She didn't have a relationship with Casey Clay.

She didn't have anything with him at all that she could possibly explain to this decent, kind man.

So what if she didn't feel bells clanging inside her and whistles blowing whenever Arlo looked her way? There were more important things. Like respect. Honesty.

A man who wanted the same things she wanted.

"It's not important," she murmured. "Just…just that I should have replaced the computer a year ago." Instead of taking Casey into her bed, she should have let him take over the computer. It would have been a lot more productive in the long run.

And a lot less painful.

"I think I'm going to need to make a trip to Gillette," she said. There was a broader selection of stores there than Weaver and Braden combined could offer. "Try to find a new one." Then there was the matter of getting everything transferred onto it from her deader-than-a-doornail antique.

Something else that Casey could have accomplished with his eyes blindfolded.

Could this man *please* stop congesting all of her thoughts?

Annoyed with herself, she pushed to her feet and stopped in front of Arlo. She was back in her comfortable cowboy boots, jeans and turtleneck sweater. She was in *her* office, on *her* turf, and a certain gray-eyed man had no business interfering.

She rested her palms lightly on Arlo's pale blue dress shirt and stretched up to press her mouth against his.

She felt his hands lift to lightly clasp her shoulders.

But that was *all* she felt.

She had no interest whatsoever in ripping off his shirt. Or finding herself flattened between his body and the storeroom door.

She lowered her heels again, wanting to rail at the universe. "You're a nice man, Arlo," she said again. Gently. "But I don't think this is going to work."

"Because you're involved with Casey Clay?"

She blinked. Arlo's easy tone hadn't changed, but she certainly hadn't expected the words. "I'm not."

"But you were."

"I thought you were an estate lawyer, not a private investigator," she said in a light tone.

He smiled ruefully. "What I am is observant. Just because I was out of town the last few days doesn't mean I don't know he went with you to your mother-in-law's funeral."

"Memorial service," she corrected him.

"And that he's been a regular…guest…at your place for some months now."

Not recently. She managed to keep her mouth shut on that one.

"Nobody knew about that. We were extremely discreet. We didn't want the town gossiping about things they knew nothing about!"

He smiled faintly. His hands were still on her arms. "Maybe you were discreet enough to duck the grapevine's radar, but that doesn't mean *everyone* was oblivious."

She made a face. "But you still asked me out."

"To be accurate, you initiated that. When you asked Hayley to give me your number."

She rubbed her forehead. "God. This is so humiliating."

He patted her shoulder comfortingly before dropping his hands. "I enjoy your company, Jane. I figured if you were willing to go out with me in the first place that Casey didn't have a lock on your time, no matter what was going on between you. You can't deny that you and I have a lot of things in common. We're after the same things. You want marriage and kids. So do I."

Which wouldn't happen through immaculate conception.

And whether or not she liked what Casey had said when she'd first shared her plan to become a mother, he had a point.

Babies usually started out if not from love, then at least from passion.

"But I don't think that's going to be in the cards for us together," she said carefully.

"Well." His smile turned rueful. "I guess that message is pretty clear."

"I'm sorry, Arlo. I wish—" She broke off when he shook his head.

"Don't be sorry. We're both old enough to know you can't pretend what you don't feel. I'd still like you to come with me on Sunday. There's never a downside to having an interesting, beautiful woman nearby."

"You're good for my ego, but going with you won't change anything."

"Yeah, well, indulge me a little. All the other lawyers who'll be there will have dates. I don't look forward to being the odd man out. You might even have a little fun. It would be something different, at least."

She exhaled and headed out of her office. She paused when she reached the swinging door that led to the bar. "I'm not sure it's a good idea, but okay."

He nodded, obviously satisfied. "I'll pick you up about noon. Dress warm." He pushed open the door for her to go through first.

Casey was standing next to the bar, bouncing his keys in the palm of his hand.

He looked terrible. As if he hadn't slept in days. His bloodshot gaze slid over Arlo, then her.

The last thing she expected was for Arlo to lean down and kiss her right on the lips, but that was what he did. Then he slid his mouth near her ear. "Keep your chin up," he murmured.

Then he straightened and gave Casey an easy smile before striding across the bar and pushing through the exit.

"Not wasting any time, I see," Casey said.

She curled her fingers until her nails dug into the palms of her hands and willed away whatever concern she felt over the fresh lines in his face and the tension pulsing out of his cells. "Just because I was stupid enough to sleep with you for the past year doesn't mean I'm a whore," she managed tightly.

He sighed. "I'm sorry. That was uncalled for. Not once have I ever thought of you like that."

She ignored him and went behind the bar, snatching up a bottle of vodka that hadn't been replaced on the shelf where it belonged. "You found your truck keys, obviously." Her chest ached so badly it was hard to get out the words. "So just take them and go."

"And if I made you feel like one—"

She closed her eyes, tightening her grip on the bottle. She didn't want to drop it, because her palm felt suddenly moist and slick. Nor did she want to heave it at his head.

Either was a distinct possibility.

"—then I deserve every crummy thing you've ever thought about me. And there aren't any apologies good enough."

She carefully set the bottle on the shelf and turned to face him. "I didn't expect to see you. Steven from the plane said you'd be sending someone to get your truck."

"I didn't expect to be here either." He didn't move from where he stood at the end of the bar but had stopped jangling the keys in his hand.

Then why are you?

And why did she hurt so badly inside because he was?

She pushed the empty register drawer closed. "How did you get back from Denver?"

"Picked up another flight."

"Cee-Vid has a bunch of planes at your disposal?"

"It wasn't Cee-Vid. But Tris does happen to have more than one." He went silent for a moment. "I didn't come for the keys. I came to tell you I'm going to be out of town for a while. A couple weeks, maybe."

"We've never kept up with each other's schedules before," she said, managing a halfway even tone.

His lips tightened. "Maybe I thought you should know. So you wouldn't think my being gone had anything to do with—"

"Me?"

He pinched the bridge of his nose, then dropped his hand. "With last night."

"Look, Casey." She pressed her palms flat on the counter in front of her, feeling the textured rubbery mat dig into her skin. "We're not lovers anymore. I think we've proven we're not friends. So let's just stop pretending there's any reason why you need to inform me of anything, much less the fact you'll be out of town for a few weeks. It doesn't matter to me what you do. Or where you are." Two bigger lies she'd never told in her life. "It was entertaining while it lasted, but it's over." She made herself shrug even though her throat was in a vise, her voice turning thin. "No harm. No foul."

"Maybe that crap flies with other people, but it doesn't with me. Not anymore. You want to stop pretending?" He suddenly moved toward her, leaning across the bar until their noses were only inches apart. "Stop pretending that we were just a convenient hookup whenever one of us had…an…itch."

Her eyes burned. "What good would that do? It doesn't get me any closer to the things I want in life!"

"A baby."

She threw up her hands, backing up until she felt the counter behind her against her spine. "Yes! A baby. I want a baby. I want a husband. And you think I didn't know that the second I said those words you'd be scoping out the closest exit? I knew, and it was exactly what happened!" Her choked voice rang out.

And it was perfectly audible for the small crowd that had formed in the archway between the grill and the bar, avid expressions on their faces.

Her shoulders fell. She lowered her hands to her sides. "Well," she muttered thickly. "I guess we can forget about keeping things just between you and me."

He barely gave their audience a glance. "I wasn't looking for an exit because I wanted to," he said flatly.

"I don't even have a clue what that's supposed to mean. I don't have a clue what goes on inside your head. Inside your heart. The only thing I know for sure about you is that your work is always, *always* going to come first."

"It means I can't give you what you want," he said between his teeth.

"You mean you won't."

"I mean I *can't*," he repeated. Then he looked at the people watching them. Even Jerry, her cook, was there, his mouth open in shock.

Casey shook his head, his eyes a stormy gray. "I can't," he said again.

Then he turned and walked out of the bar.

Chapter Ten

"So that's it." Casey stared at a photo of the ramshackle hut situated across the narrow rutted road. The satellite image blazing across the wall in front of him was so clear he could have been standing within touching distance of the hut, rather than several thousand miles away, safe inside an air-conditioned vault deep within Hollins-Winword's Connecticut compound. "That's where Jon and Manny died."

"That's it." Tristan got up from where he'd been sitting beside Casey and moved past the computer consoles to stand next to the wall of screens. Currently, the screens were working in tandem to display this one huge image, and even his oversize uncle looked small in comparison as he walked over to stand just below the hut. He stared intently, as if he could see something that Casey and the others gathered together in the room couldn't.

For the past week, the six members of the investigation team had pored over every speck of data they had concerning the three agents' activities during the months leading up to when Jon and Manny had died in that Honduran hut.

There was no evidence their cover had been blown. To anyone who'd looked, they'd been three expats cranking out a meager existence alongside the locals in a small, nearly forgotten town. Their true task had been simply to gather intel on a drug lord who'd also been dipping his toes into human trafficking. Nasty stuff. HW had been feeding evidence to the authorities who were supposed to be able to do something about the situation.

There was no hint, no sign, no anything, that explained how, when or why they'd been found out. Nothing to explain the bullets that had struck down Jon and Manny.

It had taken Casey and the rest of their team four full days just to confirm that the two men hadn't died where their bodies had been discovered, some hundred miles north near San Pedro Sula.

Whoever had killed them had moved their bodies.

Which tended to dispel the theory that the men might have died through some coincidence unrelated to their true mission.

They'd spent the rest of the week trying to unearth the truth, and failing. And now the prevailing sense Casey got from the rest of his team members was that this particular mystery wasn't going to be solved. At least, not by them.

Not until they found McGregor. Either he'd killed his partners, which seemed unfathomable, or he was in so much danger he couldn't be found.

Casey didn't like agreeing with the team's assessment. But he didn't have any basis to argue either.

"Okay." Tristan finally turned to face them. "Wrap it

up." He looked at the only female there. "Theresa, finish the report and have it to me in sixty. I want to be wheels up in sixty-five."

"Yes, sir." Theresa de Santos gathered her stack of materials and left the room, followed by the other team members.

They would be dispersing to various corners of the world. Only Casey and his uncle would head back to Weaver.

"This sucks," Casey said bluntly the second they had the room to themselves.

"Yup." His uncle agreed immediately. He stopped on the other side of the console and studied him. "Have you slept at all since we've been here?"

Not much. And not well. Every time he closed his eyes, he saw Jane's face.

Or he heard the bone-jarring sound of seven rifles being shot off at once.

"I'm fine," he said.

"You're not fine." Tristan's face was hard. "Trust me, kid. You won't be the first Clay to ever get suspended from Hollins-Winword, but that's what's going to happen if you don't pull yourself together."

"There's nothing wrong with my work." His voice was flat. "Except for losing three agents on my freaking watch, I'm as good as you ever were."

"Christ. You think I don't know that?" Tristan reached out and flicked his finger stingingly against Casey's temple. "What's wrong is in there. You're letting this eat at you from the inside, just like I warned against. You looked in a mirror lately? Maggie may be a bitty thing, but your mom'll string me up from my toes if she sees you looking like this. And I don't even want to think what your dad will do to me. You're my nephew, for God's sake. Bad enough we've already lived through Ryan's and Ax's experiences with the agency. Now it's your turn?"

He propped his hands on his hips and continued. "I swear to God, I'm never letting Cole pull anyone else I care about into this bloody business, no matter how good you are at what you do. Clean up. Take a shower, for cryin' out loud. Close the file on this. Not just here—" he flipped his hand against Casey's pile of notebooks and files, then jabbed him in the forehead even harder "—but here. Or I *will* suspend you." Then he headed out of the room.

Casey knew it wasn't an empty threat.

What would he do if he didn't have Hollins-Winword? If all he really did was keep the systems for the public face of Cee-Vid running merrily along?

There was nothing else in his life.

Yeah, he had his sisters. His parents, Daniel and Maggie. He had nieces and nephews and cousins and extended family galore.

But he couldn't make a child of his own.

He'd had to accept that failure a decade ago when the girl he'd loved tossed him out like yesterday's trash after learning he'd never be able to put the babies she wanted in her belly.

He'd been only twenty-one.

He was long over Caitlyn now. He even recognized the fact that he'd escaped what would have been a disastrous marriage.

But nothing else had changed.

He was still sterile.

He couldn't be the man—the husband—that Jane needed.

Which left him with only Hollins-Winword.

What would he do if he lost that, too?

* * *

"Vivian," Hayley said to the diminutive white-haired woman, "these are my friends, Jane Cohen and Samantha Dawson."

Hayley's grandmother beamed at them, placed her narrow hand in Jane's and shook it with surprising firmness. Then she did the same with Sam. "At least some people have been welcoming me to Wyoming."

Hayley made a face as she grabbed two unused folding chairs from the table next to theirs and brought them to the other side of the crowded banquet table where Jane and Sam were already sitting with a few others from Colbys. "Daddy and Uncle David will come around," she told Vivian. "Just have patience."

Vivian's lined face creased even more as she sat in one of the chairs. Her eyes were such a dark brown they were nearly black, but they sparkled with wry humor. "I'm eighty-six years old, dear. I don't necessarily have the luxury of patience."

It was the day after Halloween and Jane was meeting up with her girlfriends at the high school gym for the town's Harvest Festival. Half the space was given over to carnival games for children. The other half was taken up by displays of baked goods and potluck dishes.

Looking around her with unabashed curiosity, Vivian patted her stylishly coiffed hair with a hand heavily weighted by diamonds. "It's taken me much too long to come to Wyoming. It's a great deal more civilized than I pictured."

"But a long way from Pittsburgh," Jane commented.

Vivian's eyebrows lifted. "Have you been there?"

She shook her head. "Never been farther east than Chicago."

"Well, it was home," Vivian said. "It's where my

sons were all born." Her lips thinned a little as her gaze scanned the people milling around the gym. "Though they all defected to head west."

"Vivian," Hayley's voice was soft. But it held a gentle warning.

Jane and Hayley hadn't had a chance to privately discuss anything that had occurred in the past several days. But from Hayley's tone, Jane was guessing that her friend and her grandmother had had a few discussions of their own.

Vivian exhaled and twisted the enormous ring on her wedding finger. "I know." Her gaze took in Jane and Sam once more. "So does this Harvest Festival have such a thing as cocktails?"

"Afraid you'll have to wait until later," Jane said wryly. "Strictly a nonalcoholic event. But there's punch, iced tea and a pretty good lemonade. And the food—" She gestured at the lines queuing up around the offerings. "You can see nobody's sitting around on their thumbs waiting."

"Hayley, dear, get me a lemonade," Vivian said in what Jane hoped was an unconsciously superior tone, and her friend dutifully set off. "My granddaughter tells me you're a police officer, Samantha? And, Jane, you own a bar and grill?"

Sam nodded. She was never much of a conversationalist in social situations.

"Sam's the only female deputy sheriff we've got here in Weaver," Jane added.

"Really." Vivian gave Sam an approving look. "Good for you, dear. In my day women usually only worked until they found themselves a husband." She pressed her palm to the front of her pink nubby silk jacket. "Or in my case, husbands."

"Not all at the same time," Hayley interjected on a

laugh as she set a plastic cup filled with lemonade on the table in front of her grandmother and sat down.

Vivian laughed, too. "Good heavens, no. I *tried* to leave the scandals in the family to others, though my first husband, Hayley's grandfather, seemed to want to thwart my effort at every turn. Four," she said abruptly. "Four husbands. One after the other." Her gaze drifted a little. "I buried them all, sadly. Punishment for my misdeeds, I'm sure." She refocused her attention on Jane and Sam. "Are you girls single, like Hayley? No husbands yet?"

Jane buried her nose in her iced tea, leaving Sam to answer. Since Casey had left town, the thought of husbands had become alarmingly unappealing.

"By the time I was your age," Vivian reminisced, "I had three sons already in elementary school."

Jane glanced at Hayley. She'd heard her friend speak of only her dad and one uncle.

"Thatcher was the oldest," Hayley provided. "Then Uncle David."

"Then Hayley's father, Carter, was the youngest." Vivian looked sad. "Thatcher died in a skiing accident when he was a young man. I thought he was destined to be a musician. The finest. My own father was a violin maker and Thatcher's father played beautifully—that's how we met. But all Thatcher wanted was adventure." Then with an obvious effort, her expression perked up, and she picked up her plastic cup, which looked rather incongruous in her heavily ringed fingers. "To family," she said, determinedly cheerful. "Ones lost and ones rediscovered."

"To family," they all murmured, and touched their cups together.

Jane hoped her face didn't show just how hollow the words made her feel.

Aside from Julia off in Montana, Jane had no family.

Considering the state of things with the only man she seemed to want, she feared she never would.

"So—" Vivian set her cup down and closed her hand around Hayley's "—tell me about Weaver." The older woman's gaze roved around. She was clearly not ashamed of being caught people-watching. "Who's who and all of that?"

Jane was guessing Vivian's suit was Chanel. That, along with her flashing jewels, made her stick out like a sore thumb among the sea of people dressed in blue jeans, flannel shirts and cowboy hats. But if she liked gossip, she'd fit right in.

"That's the sheriff over there," Hayley was saying, nodding toward the tall dark-haired man studying the selection of pies being judged for the bake-off. "Max Scalise."

"Handsome," Vivian murmured. "Married?"

"Yes," Hayley drawled, "and too young for Husband Number Five anyway."

Vivian chuckled. "I'm done with marriage, dear," she assured them. "The years I got to have with Arthur, my last husband," she said, looking at Sam and Jane, "were more perfect than any woman deserved. Particularly me. He was a good, good man. I'm not on a quest to try and replicate what can't be replicated." She gave Hayley a look. "I do, however, want to right some old wrongs, an effort your father and uncle seem determined to thwart."

"Give them time."

From the corner of her eye, Jane saw Casey's parents, Maggie and Daniel, enter the gym. She sat forward, propping her elbows on the table. As far as she knew, Casey was still out of town, but that didn't stop her nerves from ratcheting up several notches. "How long were you and

Arthur married, Mrs. Templeton?" She thought it strange that the woman had had three husbands after Hayley's grandfather but still used her first husband's name.

"Ten years. Just ten years." She let go of Hayley's hand and fiddled with her rings. "The punishment of a foolish old woman. I could have had a lot longer with him if not for my own pride." She leaned closer. "Arthur was a retired history teacher," she confided, as if it were something secretive. "Not a professor, mind you. He taught children. In *public school*."

Sam stirred. "There are worse things."

"Of course there are, dear." Vivian sat back again. "But old habits died hard. He came from a different class. I used to think things like that mattered. But Arthur changed all that."

Jane realized she was watching the door for Casey and looked away. "How did the two of you meet?"

"Gardening. Arthur had a prize collection of roses."

"So does my grandmother," Hayley added. "She has a rose garden you wouldn't believe back in Pittsburgh. She's been showing me photographs."

"Sawyer—that's Hayley's grandfather—he planted the roses himself," Vivian said. "They're still beautiful all these years later." Her gaze drifted past Jane and Sam again. "He was always a nurturing soul," she murmured. "Who's *that*?"

Jane glanced over her shoulder and her stomach dropped away as her gaze collided with Casey's.

She'd thought he'd looked terrible the week before, but he looked even worse now.

Not that Vivian seemed to see anything amiss. Nor did Hayley or Sam, it seemed.

Maybe she was the only one to recognize the way the

lines arrowing out from his eyes were deeper, the way the set of his lips was thinner. Grimmer.

He'd entered along with his grandparents, Squire and Gloria Clay, and a bunch of other relatives. Everyone headed en masse toward several tables on the other side of the room.

Everyone except Casey.

He was headed her way.

"That's Casey Clay," she heard Hayley tell Vivian as he approached. "He's Jane's beau, though they both deny it."

Jane sent her friend a look that Hayley ignored.

"Good heavens, not the *young* one," Vivian said impatiently. "The white-haired one. With the steely face and the walking stick."

"You mean Mr. Clay? Squire Clay," Sam provided. "The Clays own one of the largest cattle operations in the state. The Double-C. He's married, too," she added humorously.

Jane was barely listening to their exchange. She pushed out of her chair and muttered an excuse that she needed the restroom before Casey reached their table.

Then, feeling like the biggest coward on the planet, she hustled her butt in the opposite direction.

But she felt him on her heels even before she pushed through the double swinging doors that led from the gymnasium, and as soon as she was in the mercifully empty corridor on the other side, she halted, rounding on him. "What do you want?"

He stopped short, too, his eyes narrowing. "Why'd you run?"

If he could ignore her question, she could ignore his. "Guess your trip didn't take as long as you expected. You look like you haven't slept since you left in the first place.

What were you doing, anyway? Taking care of some vitally important Cee-Vid disaster at one of the other sites?"

His lips tightened. "You sell booze and food. I'm pretty sure that means you're not against entertainment. So what do you have against Cee-Vid? People get a lot of entertainment from the games they produce."

"*They* produce." She crossed her arms.

"What?"

"They produce," she repeated. "They, they, they! Shouldn't you be saying *we*? You spend all of your time devoted to that company, but you don't even claim a bit of ownership over what Cee-Vid does."

He stared at her as if she'd lost her mind.

Which she was fairly certain she had done a year ago, when they'd kissed the first time.

"What the hell are you going on about?"

She yanked on the collar of her turtleneck, which had been perfectly comfortable before he'd arrived but now seemed to be strangling her. She'd never expected him to be at the Harvest Festival, or she would have begged off when Hayley and Sam suggested going. "I don't know," she snapped. "You're making me crazy."

"Well, that makes us even," he returned, not sounding any happier about the situation. He pulled a folded envelope out of his back pocket and handed it to her.

She took it cautiously, thinking too easily about the note he'd left her in Denver. The note she still hadn't thrown away. "What's this?"

"Registration for your pool tournament."

Of course. There was no accounting for the disappointment that settled like a stone inside her stomach. It wasn't as if she expected anything else from him. She unfolded the envelope and looked inside, seeing the registration form and his personal check. "Personal delivery wasn't necessary, you know."

"I didn't have a postage stamp," he said flatly. "If you didn't insist on living in the dark ages, you'd have it so people could register online. I could have set it all up for you in five minutes."

"I like tradition," she returned. "Remember?"

"Speaking of. Where's Arlo?"

"He's coming later," she lied. She had no idea what Arlo's plans were, though she had no intention of telling Casey that. Even though Arlo had been as bored with the uptight picnic she'd accompanied him to as she had been, they hadn't gone out again since.

His lips tightened. "It's going well, then. This 'get a husband, get a baby' plan of yours."

Her chest ached. "Let's just say I'm not taking my birth control pills anymore." She wanted to rescind the words the second they escaped, but they were already out there. Seeming to echo around the tiled corridor.

A curtain came down in his gray eyes, making them more unreadable than ever, and the silence between them tightened unbearably, broken only by a sudden burst of laughter from the other side of the swinging doors.

"I guess congratulations are in order," he said then. His tanned face looked unnaturally pale. "What're you sending out first? The wedding invitations or the birth announcements?"

She swallowed. Her mouth felt arid and she rocked uncomfortably on her heels. "Neither. Yet," she hedged, wondering when she'd become such a liar. Wondering if the trait had lurked inside her all of her life, or if it had bloomed only as a result of protecting herself against what she couldn't have.

Him.

"But I'm…hopeful." Which was the biggest lie of all.

Because where she and Casey Clay were concerned, there was no hope.

In her head, she'd known it all along and it was long past time she convinced her heart of it, too.

Chapter Eleven

"Merilee, have you seen the list of the table monitors?"

Her assistant manager was setting up on the sidewalk outside Colbys where the pool tournament entrants would begin checking in later that day. She squinted against the cold December sunlight as she looked at Jane. "Last I saw, it was on the desk in your office." In one hand, she held a bundle of artificial garland, and in the other, a large plastic bag filled with round Christmas-tree ornaments. "Do you want me to hang more of this stuff, or get started on the tree decorations?"

Jane had hired a group from the high school to hang the deep green garland that festooned the front of her building, and Merilee had already strung smaller additional strands in the windows, around the doors and from the registration table. Similar holiday decor graced nearly every building up and down Main. The park across the street on the corner had set up dozens and dozens of

Christmas trees in anticipation of the community tree lighting the following day and everything around town was spit-shined and bright in preparation.

She realized Merilee was still waiting for an answer. "Get started on the trees," she said as she pulled open the door to go inside. "Let me know if you run out of bulbs. I bought extra."

She'd rearranged everything in the bar to accommodate some of the additional pool tables she'd brought in to handle the load of the tournament. Since it still hadn't snowed yet, she'd decided to use the parking lot between Colbys and the dance studio for the rest of the tables. The extra tables were set up beneath a tent and cordoned off from the street by a row of narrow Douglas firs that would soon be decked out with Merilee's ornaments.

Jane had more than a hundred players coming in for the tournament that would start that afternoon and, for the first time ever, would spill over to the next day. She'd promised Weaver's overly cautious council that she would be finished well before the town's Advent season officially kicked off with the tree-lighting celebration, and she wanted everything to go well. If it didn't, she figured there'd be pressure from the council to drop ideas of a repeat next year.

She had no intention of letting that happen, though. She'd planned too hard and too long. Her storeroom shelves were fully stocked. Both the grill and the bar had an extra contingent of servers scheduled to be on hand. Everything was set and ready to go. Not only would the winners of the tournament go home with their pocketbooks loaded, the charities in Weaver would benefit, and Colbys would rake in a huge profit on increased food and drink sales.

It was a win-win situation all the way around.

But she'd never felt less like celebrating.

She found the list of table monitors she'd been look-ing for right where Merilee said it was.

In Jane's office. On her desk.

Sitting in plain sight, where she ought to have seen it if she'd only been able to concentrate.

Disgusted with herself, she sat down at her desk in front of the fancy new computer she'd purchased. It pos-sessed every bell and whistle that Casey had ever insisted she needed.

She'd hired a guy from the store in Gillette where she'd purchased it to come and set it up for her. Unfor-tunately, the thing was so different from her old com-puter that aside from turning it on, she hardly knew how to operate it.

Sighing, she focused on the volunteer list. She'd had Olive make reminder calls to everyone on it regarding their time slots. She knew from experience that there were always a few people who'd back out for various reasons, but there had been only one. She carried the list out to the huge corkboard she'd placed against one wall and pinned it there for everyone to see. It would be a simple double-elimination tournament played as much for fun and bragging rights as anything else, and as the games progressed, she'd update the oversize bracket she'd printed out that was fixed high on the wall above the corkboard.

Everything was set.

All they needed now was for the participants to show up. Play would begin at noon and they could start check-ing in ninety minutes before that.

Which still gave Jane an hour.

An hour when she didn't have enough busywork to keep her mind consumed.

She wandered into the grill but as soon as she showed her face in the kitchen, Jerry pointed his spatula at the door. "Out. Don't mess with me today," he warned. His tone was good-natured enough, but his eyes said he wasn't joking. "Don't need you telling me how to do things I been doing since you were in diapers."

She lifted her hands in a placating gesture. "I'm not here to tell you how to do your job," she insisted.

He harrumphed and expertly flipped the eggs he was frying. "Then whatcha doing in my kitchen?"

It was her kitchen, actually. She owned it, after all. But pointing that out would likely make her cook quit on what she expected would be one of her busiest weekends of the year.

"Just wanted to see your smiling face, Jer. Make sure you have everything you need for this weekend."

"You saying I don't know how to plan for a big crowd?"

She tossed up her hands, giving up. "Keep your apron on, all right? I'm leaving your sacred space." She backed out through the swinging doors.

About a third of the tables in the restaurant were occupied, mostly by unfamiliar faces.

Townies almost always went to Ruby's. And even though the café was her competition, she could hardly blame them. Not when it came to breakfast.

But for lunch? She was in a dead heat with Ruby's. And dinner was a no-brainer since the other restaurant closed after lunch and didn't even offer it.

There wasn't a single thing she could do in the bar to ready it more than it already was, so she pulled on her jacket and went back outside. Merilee was busy hanging red-and-white Christmas balls on the trees and Jane went to help.

Before long, they had dolled up the half-dozen trees. Soon after, the first of the players started arriving, so Jane went over to get them checked in while Merilee made sure the outdoor heaters were keeping the area beneath the tent comfortable.

The first players were quickly followed by more, and before long, Jane was neck-deep in checking people in, taking registration money from those who still owed it and handing out copies of the rules.

It was only a matter of time before one member or another of the Clay family showed up.

She was just glad that it wasn't Casey who did so first. She hadn't seen him since that afternoon at the Harvest Festival.

Five weeks ago. He hadn't been to Colbys once in five weeks. Not to play pool with his family, though they'd made regular appearances. Not to eat in the restaurant.

She knew he hadn't been out of town again either, because she'd seen his familiar black pickup more than once on the street.

The message was clear. She'd told him they were done, and despite their missteps along the way, ever since the Harvest Festival, he'd obviously decided he agreed.

Now, after she'd told herself day in and day out that it was all for the best, the idea of being face-to-face with him again had her in knots.

She checked in his cousin Sarah, who was married to the sheriff and taught over at the elementary school. She checked in his sister J.D. She checked in Erik. And Axel. More cousins. Even his father, Daniel, who looked so much like a future version of Casey that it was painful.

Along with the portable heaters in the parking lot, they'd also rigged up speakers from the bar's jukebox. They'd turn the volume down some as soon as the tournament started, but for now, country music blared, alternating with Christmas carols. To this accompaniment, for ninety minutes she registered people she knew and people she didn't know. By noon she'd handed out almost every packet she'd prepared for the players and there was still no sign of him.

Were things so irrevocably ruined that he'd blow off the tournament?

She was ready to give up and head inside when she saw him. Striding down the street alongside Tristan, and her heart climbed right into her throat.

He stopped in front of the table. She handed him the packet.

And that was it.

He silently took the envelope without touching her fingers and went inside.

She swallowed hard, schooling her expression, and looked up at his uncle as she passed him the last envelope. Whether Casey had wanted her to or not, she *had* mailed Tristan Clay a thank-you note weeks ago for the use of his plane when Althea died. But there was another matter that she had never addressed. "I was sorry to hear about the two employees you lost a few months ago," she said now.

The tall man's vivid blue gaze settled on her face, making her feel oddly uncomfortable. As if she'd treaded in waters she shouldn't have.

"Casey told me," she added quickly. "Not, uh, not what happened. An accident, I assume, but—"

"Thank you," Tristan cut off her awkward words. He didn't smile exactly, but something in his eyes softened. "Casey's taking what happened pretty hard."

Her discomfort rose to new heights, since she had

no idea at all what had happened. She just knew he was right; the effect of the accident on Casey had been severe.

"Anyway, I wanted to tell you I was sorry." She had no more registrants coming, so she hopped to her feet and yanked open the door for him, anxious to go inside, where it was warmer.

"Thanks." He started to go in but hesitated. "Are you going to be tied up here all weekend?"

"Until the winners are decided." She pinned on a smile. "On which note I should wish you good luck at the tables. Seems like half the players are relatives of yours. I'm glad none of you minds some healthy competition with each other, or I'd only have half the players that I do."

He smiled faintly. "*Healthy* might be overstating it. But judging by the crowd you've got, I think we'd need another generation of kids before there'd be enough of us to make up half."

Her insides squeezed, but she kept her smile in place.

"We'll all be over at the park for the tree lighting tomorrow evening. Come and join us if you can. My brother Matt insists it's finally going to snow and he's almost always right when it comes to snow."

It was a casual invitation. Surely nothing more than what he would extend to anyone. But her gaze still flicked past him, searching out Casey. The pool tables were numbered for the tournament. She'd assigned the players to each one herself. It was easy to find him. She started to shake her head. "That's nice of you, but I—"

"Don't give up on him," Tristan interrupted quietly.

Her mouth went a little dry. He obviously knew about loaning them his own company plane. But beyond that? Did he know only what the rest of the town thought they knew about her and Casey?

Did he know that a person couldn't give up on something that never existed in the first place?

"I—" She broke off and cleared the constriction from her throat with a soft cough. "It's complicated."

The older man's lips twitched. "It always is." He touched her elbow lightly as he passed. "Say you'll think about it at least."

Despite knowing it was the last thing she should do, she nodded. "I'll think about it."

"Good girl." He actually gave her a wink, so quick she wasn't sure she hadn't imagined it, and headed into the crowd packed inside the bar, hailing people along the way.

She watched his progress for a moment, then couldn't keep from looking Casey's way.

He was looking at her.

But as soon as their gazes collided, he turned his back.

She inhaled slowly, then forced herself to go inside.

Casey or no Casey, she had a pool tournament to run.

Casey lost his first game, much to the hoots and hollers of his supposedly loyal family.

Worse, he lost to a high school kid who was still wet behind his ears.

He shook the kid's hand and left the table, pool cue metaphorically tucked between his legs as he headed to the corner of the bar where some of his family was clustered. "Yeah, yeah. No comments from the peanut gallery," he said when he joined them.

"Didn't look like your mind was where it needed to be, son." His father, Daniel, was at a high-top table with Casey's uncles and their father, Squire. He was nursing a longneck beer and looking gleeful. Probably because his name was already ahead of Casey's on the brackets, since he'd won *his* first time out.

In fact, when Casey looked over at the big chart that Jane was constantly updating as the tournament progressed, he could see that all of the Clays who'd played so far had won their games.

"Might've helped if you'd been studying the table and not that pretty girl's rear view," Squire added.

Despite himself, Casey looked toward Jane.

In honor of the season she had on snug white jeans and a red turtleneck that clung to every curve she possessed.

He wasn't the only one who'd been noticing her.

Every time she climbed up on her ladder to write in the latest results on the brackets, some fool—like him—managed to blow his shot. One guy at the table next to him had even jumped the cue ball right over the side rail.

"Though she does have a real pretty…er…view," Squire added, watching Jane climb up the short ladder. She had a notepad in her hand that she consulted before she uncapped her thick black marker and added another line of perfectly printed letters to the chart.

There was just something unnatural about a person who printed so neatly. It was freakish in comparison to his own scrawl.

He dragged his gaze away from the way her butt filled out her jeans and propped his cue stick against his dad's table. "Gonna go see how Erik and Ax are doing," he muttered.

They were somewhere outside at the pool tables under the tent. Casey wished he were, too. Merilee was keeping track of the scores outside, and she wouldn't have posed a distraction to him at all.

He worked his way around the congested room, thinking it was probably a good thing the sheriff was participating in the tournament, too, since Jane was definitely over the maximum occupancy. Max wasn't likely to give her a ticket for the infraction when he was part of the reason.

Before Casey made it to the exit, he saw her step back down the ladder and move behind the bar.

She had four bartenders there already. As far as he could tell, they hadn't stopped to breathe since the pool playing commenced a good three hours earlier. That didn't stop her from getting in there, mixing a few and— if he knew her—telling them how to do what they were already doing.

Jane liked things the way Jane liked things.

He made it through the door into the cold afternoon and headed down the sidewalk toward the parking lot.

The space between Jane's building and Lucy's dance studio was more congested with players and onlookers than the bar had been, and with the portable heaters, it seemed even warmer.

He was no more in the mood to wade through the melee here than he had been to show up for the tournament at all.

The only reason he *had* was because it gave him an excuse to see Janie.

Didn't matter that it was pointless.

She was through with him. She was seeing Arlo.

For the past month, everywhere he turned, he heard ad nauseam about how Arlo'd taken to having lunch every day at Colbys. How they'd spent Thanksgiving together and his car was parked in front of her condo all the time now.

Whether Casey liked it or not, Arlo was the kind of man she wanted. Openly. Publicly.

He was the kind whose work never called him away

at inopportune moments. Whose work was exactly what Arlo said it was. He wouldn't do what her ex-husband had done—constantly put her second. And he would do what Casey couldn't—give her the baby she wanted.

Every day he woke, he expected to hear they were making it official. And every night when he went to bed without hearing it, he hated the selfish relief he felt.

With his mood growing even more sour, he turned and headed across the street to the park instead. There were already preparations under way for tomorrow's tree lighting. Tables had been set up for the covered dishes everyone brought for the potluck supper—nothing more than big sheets of plywood propped over barrels that would get sheets of red-and-green plastic for tablecloths. There were tall propane heaters to hold the cold at bay and folding chairs set out near the pavilion for the bands that would play. Nobody bothered putting up a dance floor. If people had a mind to dance, they would, right there on the frost-browned grass, among the dozens of Christmas trees that were being strung with lights.

The world kept ticking along whether he liked it or not.

He scrubbed his cold hand over his face and wandered around the pavilion. It was almost funny to see the couple in a clinch in the shadows behind the circular structure. For as long as he could remember, kids had used that spot to make out.

He'd been guilty of it a time or two himself back when he'd been in school.

But as he turned away before they noticed him, he recognized the man. And it was no longer funny.

Arlo Bellamy was playing tonsil hockey with a woman very clearly *not* Jane.

Casey cleared his throat and the couple sprang apart. He didn't know her name, but he recognized the woman—dark haired and young—from Shop-World, where she was a clerk. Her identity didn't mean diddly to Casey, except to know she wasn't Jane. "Couldn't find a spot that offered a little more privacy?"

The other man didn't even have the grace to look ashamed. He kept his arm slung over the girl's shoulder. "You know how it is, Casey." His tone was easy. Friendly. As if they'd run into each other outside the hardware store and had stopped to shoot the breeze. "When the moment strikes and all."

Casey saw red and his fist balled, flashing out to plant square in Arlo's face. Arlo's head bounced back, blood spurting from his nose.

The girl screamed and raced away, running hell-bent for leather across the street.

Casey didn't give her a thought. "You know how it is," he told Arlo through his teeth. "When the moment strikes and all."

Arlo had covered his face with his hand and was sidling sideways away from Casey. "Are you *crazy*? What the hell's wrong with you? I'm bleeding like a stuck pig!"

Casey sidestepped along with him. They were toe to toe. "If the shoe fits. What the hell's wrong with *you*? You think you can treat her like this?"

"Amber? She's—"

"*Jane*," he said through clenched teeth. "I'm talking about Jane."

Blood was dripping down Arlo's chin. Onto his coat. He eyed Casey over his hand as if he'd lost his mind.

Maybe he had. He hadn't punched someone since he was fifteen and full of teenage bravado and stupidity.

"She's got nothing to do with this," Arlo said.

Fresh fury coursed through Casey, and his fist curled

again, but someone grabbed his shoulder from behind before he could do more than that. "Hold on there, hoss."

Casey jerked around to find Max. The girl, Amber, had obviously run him down from the tournament. She was panting, holding her side, as she warily circled Casey to get to Arlo's side.

"This doesn't concern you, Max."

His cousin-in-law gave him a hard look. "That remains to be seen," he said evenly, and transferred his gaze to Arlo. "We gonna all go to our corners here, Arlo, or what?"

"He assaulted him," Amber insisted. Her hands fluttered around Arlo's hands, only succeeding in smearing the blood farther. "I was right here and saw it all!"

"Mischief I break up behind the pavilion usually involves kids," Max muttered. "Not grown men old enough to know better. Arlo, you want me to take you over to the hospital? You want to file charges? What?"

"Charges." Casey nearly choked on the word. "He's cheating on Janie. A bloody nose is the least of his worries."

"You hear that?" Amber pointed her finger accusingly. "He just threatened you, Arlo! Sheriff, *do* something about him!"

Arlo lifted his hand. "Let's just all calb down," he said thickly. "Nobody's cheating and nobody's charging."

"You had your tongue down her throat," Casey snapped.

"*What* is going on here?"

They all turned to see Jane storming toward them, looking furious. Her gaze swept over Casey, then Arlo, and she paled. "Good Lord."

"Broke by dose," Arlo said. His eyes were already

looking swollen and bruised as his voice turned even more nasal. "Nudding fadal."

"He needs a doctor," Amber yelled at Max. "Why aren't you getting him to a doctor?"

Arlo patted the air again. "Calb down."

"She's right," Jane said, looking determined. "You should see a doctor, Arlo." Giving Casey a sideways look, she brushed between them and slid her arm around the other man's waist. "I have at least four of them playing pool across the street. Come on."

Amber's jaw dropped. She obviously didn't like being displaced quite so easily. She skipped along with them, doing her best to put her arm around Arlo, too.

Feeling dark inside, Casey watched them go.

"Looks like your knuckles are bleeding, too," Max observed after a moment.

Not as badly as Arlo's nose. Casey swiped them over his jeans. "You going to arrest me or something?"

"I could." Max studied him. "Don't even need Arlo to file a charge against you. Public brawling?" He shrugged. "Good enough cause. That what you want? Spend a little time in my jail cell?"

Casey grimaced. What he wanted had just walked away from him, tenderly yet bossily tending to a man who, it turned out, also didn't deserve her. "No," he answered.

"Want to tell me what happened?"

"No." He flexed his fingers. They were stiff.

"Okay." Max rubbed his chin. "So here's what you're going to do. You're going to go home. You're not going back to the tournament today. Last thing I want is that crowd over there picking up sides if that little girl, Amber, succeeds in stirring them up. Stay away from Arlo for a few days. Then apologize."

Casey spit out an oath. "He's a cheat. I'm not apologizing."

"Guess that's up to you. You might think about it, though. Arlo changes his mind about making a charge, there's nothing I can do to stop him. You want me to give you a ride home?"

"Afraid I won't follow orders?"

"Will you?"

He deliberately unclenched his jaw.

Max evidently took his silence as assent. "And get some sleep," he advised. "You look like hell."

"But I won't have a couple of black eyes," he muttered.

Max looked vaguely amused. "Of all of you Clays, I always figured you were the most peaceable. You play the violin, for God's sake."

Casey grimaced. His grandmother's violin was still broken, sitting in silent accusation on his kitchen table. "Yeah, well, I don't like cheats."

Then he turned and headed home. The fact that his uncle was sitting in one of the rocking chairs on his front porch by the time he got there wasn't a particular surprise.

"I told you to get your crap together," Tristan greeted him.

If Casey hadn't had as much respect for him as he did, he would have told him to go to hell. And damn the consequences.

"You decked an innocent man."

Casey clenched his jaw. Arlo wasn't innocent, but he knew there was no point in arguing with his uncle.

"I need you showing clear judgment," Tristan went on, pushing to his feet. "Ever since Jon's and Manny's deaths, you've been spiraling. And it stops now."

Even though he was braced for the lecture, the words felt like his fist must have felt to Arlo.

"As of now, you're suspended. You still show up at Cee-Vid. You still keep up the front. But your access to Control is cut off."

He felt another notch chip away from his world. "For how long?"

"Until I see you start acting like the man I know you are," his uncle said flatly. "If you need a counselor—"

"What the hell would I say? I can't sleep because of a few bad freaking dreams? Like I'm some little kid afraid of the damn bogey monster? I've been in Connecticut enough already. I have no desire to go back and get my head poked and prodded."

Tristan sighed. "You wouldn't have to go back there. You could see someone here. Dr. Templeton—"

"Hayley?" He let out a snort. "Sure. I'm gonna confess all to Janie's best friend. Great idea."

"She's a professional," Tristan said impatiently. "And she's heard things from more people than your smart ass knows about."

Casey ground his teeth together again, because whether he liked it or not, his uncle definitely had the right to make the call he was making.

"But if I were you," Tristan finished, "I'd start talking to the person who's a major part of your problem. I know you told Jane about Jon and Manny, so don't bother claiming she doesn't matter to you. A lot. For now, Jason McGregor is in the wind. But Jane Cohen is right here in Weaver. So stop screwing it up!"

It was nearly 2:00 a.m. when Jane parked her truck in Casey's driveway.

She was as riddled with misgivings now as she had been the first time she'd come here.

But she hadn't been able to make herself go home after

the last of the revelers and pool players called it a night. If she hadn't closed things down on them, her register would have been still ringing up drinks.

But enough was enough. She'd issued the last call, made sure everything was set for the final rounds of the pool tournament tomorrow and locked Colbys up.

She got out of the truck and walked around to the front of his darkened house. As late as it was, Casey was probably asleep. No doubt, he'd have plenty of caustic things to say if she woke him up.

She'd worn tennis shoes in anticipation of the long day and they were silent on the brick walkway. The porch light that had been turned on the last time she'd come here was dark. Casey's truck was parked in the driveway, so she assumed he was there. But the total lack of light made her wonder. She had only the moonlight to go by and was relieved when she made it up the porch steps without tripping over them. Unfortunately, once she was on the porch, the awning blocked out what little bit of light there was.

Moving blindly forward, she felt the doorknob. It had been unlocked the last time, and she was tempted to try.

But she tapped her cold knuckles on the door instead.

"You think anybody inside would hear that timid little knock?"

She was so startled by his voice coming out of the dark her heartbeat nearly exploded from her ears. "Dammit, Casey! Do you like scaring the living daylights out of me?" She peered along the dark porch and finally made out the shape of him sitting in one of the rocking chairs.

"I live here, sport. You're the one skulking around in the middle of the night."

"I'm not skulking." She folded her arms over her chest.

She'd layered a thick long-sleeved sweater over her turtle-neck once the sun had gone down, but she still felt cold.

Or maybe she was just feeling that way because she was here. With Casey. And his tone didn't hold the least bit of welcome.

"It's almost two in the morning," she pointed out. "Why aren't you in bed?"

"Why aren't you?"

"Because I just finished working for the night!"

"You think you're the only one?"

She exhaled, struggling for patience. The man excelled at frustrating her. "Don't you have any light?"

"Yes. And if I wanted any, I'd have it. What do you want, Jane?"

She wished she knew. "I just wanted to see if you were all right."

She heard a rustle, then saw him rise from the chair. "Aside from a few split knuckles, I am…just…dandy." His words were clipped.

She stiffened her spine as he stepped closer and came into focus. "What you *are* is darned lucky, Casey. Even though you broke his nose but good, Arlo isn't going to press charges."

"I don't give a damn what Arlo does or doesn't do. As long as he's not *doing* you."

"Don't be vulgar."

"Don't be naive. He was kissing someone else. Doesn't that matter to you?"

She exhaled noisily. "Arlo's free to kiss whoever he wants. We're not involved."

"That's not what you said the last time we talked."

She peered into his face. It was too dark to see his expression clearly, though even if they'd been standing beneath a spotlight, his expressions were still a mystery more often than not. "We're not going out. We never really did."

"That's not what I've been hearing around town. Why has his car been parked at your condo at night?"

"Ohmygod. You're jealous." The realization hit, and for some reason, she felt utterly incensed. She reached out and pushed his chest. "How *dare* you be jealous!"

He circled her wrists with his fingers, holding them tight. "You didn't answer the question."

She almost stomped her foot and her voice rose. "Because it doesn't deserve an answer!"

From somewhere nearby, a dog started barking. Across the street, a porch light went on.

She lowered her voice again. "I'm not the only one who lives in that complex," she reminded him tightly. "Does it occur to you that he might have been visiting someone else?"

"And this is the guy you want to have a kid with?" His voice was just as tight. "You ended a marriage because your husband spent too much time on his career. But you'll contemplate having a child with a guy who cheats on you. Why aren't *you* jealous? Or did good ol' Arlo somehow convince you that he was giving Amber some platonic little peck?"

She knew she had only herself to blame. She'd implied she was more involved with Arlo than she was.

A door had opened beneath the porch light across the street, and an old man wearing a thick robe was peering out. "Can we just go inside and have this conversation with a little more privacy instead of waking up your whole neighborhood?"

"You're the one yelling."

She jerked on her wrists, but Casey held fast. "I'm not yelling now," she said through her teeth. "Let me go."

He released her wrists so quickly she had to take a steadying step backward. "I lied, all right? I am not involved with Arlo," she repeated. "Not emotionally. Not romantically. Not involved. Period. So if you felt some… some *ridiculous* need to punch him in the face on my behalf, then I'm sorry."

"Are you sleeping with him?"

Her blood pressure rose, right along with her voice. The tips of her tennis shoes butted against his boots. "What did I just say?"

"Not emotionally. Not romantically. Not involved. Period." He was towering over her and he leaned his head toward her. "Might as well be describing us. Yet *we* were sleeping together right up until you called it quits."

"That's because I—" She broke off. *Fell in love with you.*

"Because you what?"

She shivered. "Hadn't realized I wanted more," she managed. She backed up a step. Put some breathing room between them, hoping she'd start thinking clearly again.

The man across the street had left his porch and was standing in the middle of his yard, looking right and left. The dog was still barking.

Jane let out a careful breath. "I'm not sleeping with Arlo. Not now. Not ever. I should have learned my lesson back in October. I shouldn't have come here again."

"But you did."

She was appalled to find tears burning behind her eyes. "Yup. And I am a world-class idiot for thinking that maybe, just maybe, there was some reason why I should worry about you." Her nose started running and she swiped it with her sleeve. It was utterly inelegant. She sniffed again, waving her arm out. "But you're Casey Clay. Mr. I'm-Allergic-to-Commitment. No ties. No—"

"Are you crying?"

"No!" She actually did stomp her foot at that. "And I certainly wouldn't cry because of you."

"Jesus," he muttered, and slid his palm unerringly behind her neck. "Shut the hell up."

Then he covered her mouth with his.

Chapter Twelve

Jane sucked in a sharp breath, absorbing the familiar, familiar taste of him. "This isn't right," she mumbled against him.

"Feels pretty right to me." His hand slid down her spine, hauling her closer, until she could feel the heat of him burning through her clothes. Her skin. Warming her deep inside where she'd felt cold since the last time he'd touched her. He caught the back of her head with his other hand, slanting his mouth over hers once more.

It felt as though fireworks were going off inside her. Her hands were caught between them and she worked her palms up his chest, which was hard even through the thick jacket he was wearing. She felt the charging beat of his heart. The rough inhale he took when he dragged his lips away, which she soon felt burning along her jaw. Then the side of her neck.

Her knees turned weak and he must have known it,

because he suddenly lifted her off her feet, one arm going under her rear.

The world seemed to dip and sway until she realized he was just swiveling around, fumbling for the door that opened with a loud thud as he practically stumbled through it.

A tiny part of her brain heard the dog still barking. The man across the street calling out, "Who's out there?"

But the rest of her brain just shut down as Casey pulled her into the dark foyer that went even darker when he shoved the door closed again, shutting out the barking and the old man, and pressed her flat against it.

Then it was only them.

The sounds of their breaths, nearly as loud as the pulse pounding inside her head, as the soft clank of his belt buckle when she finally managed to pull it apart.

It was so deeply dark that she couldn't have seen her own hand if she'd waved it in front of her face. But she could feel.

And touch.

The cotton knit of his shirt was soft beneath her fingers when she delved beneath his jacket and dragged it upward, out of his jeans and out of her way so she could plunge downward, shoving denim and cotton aside in favor of hot satin-skinned sinew and muscle. "Hurry," she breathed.

"I'm trying." His hands were just as busy, bunching her sweater up and yanking her jeans down her hips. "You've got on too many clothes." His mouth lowered to the skin he revealed.

She shrugged her shoulders, getting rid of the layered sweaters, and kicked the jeans off, then gasped when he tore her panties right off with a snap of the thin elastic. She cried out when he lifted her again and sank into her.

He pressed his forehead against hers, his heaving chest plastering her against the wooden door. "That fast enough for you?"

She didn't know whether to laugh or to cry but couldn't do either anyway because he was hot and hard and filling her to overflowing, and her own cells didn't seem to belong to her anymore. She wrapped her legs around him, unable to keep from greedily arching against him as much as the immovable door and his weight against her would allow. "Almost." She twined her arms around his shoulders, sinking her fingers into his thick hair, the strands cool and silky. "Almost."

His fingers tightened as he hitched her higher, thrusting harder. "Now?"

She nodded, unable to speak, unable to do anything but hold on tight as the fireworks slid from her mind into her bloodstream and exploded in a shower of brilliance, eclipsing everything else except the knowledge that he was right with her every step of the way.

She was still shuddering, breathing hard, when he finally levered away, letting her legs slowly lower until her feet found the floor.

His hand slid from her thigh to the small of her back and his head found her shoulder while he hauled in a huge, long breath. Let it out slowly. "Seems like we started out this way."

She had no difficulty at all remembering. Their first time together. In her storeroom at Colbys. After they'd been arguing about her computer.

They'd gone from squabbling to ecstasy in the blink of an eye and for the first time in her life, Jane had understood how wars could be fought over the seemingly simple matter of sex.

"Did I hurt you?"

She shook her head. It felt as weak as the rest of her. But she managed not to slither to the floor in a puddle of mush when he straightened and peeled away from her.

Without his shoulders to hold on to, she pressed her hands against the solidity of the door behind her for support. He was moving away and a moment later, bright light assaulted her from the fixture hanging over the foyer.

She blinked, shading her eyes.

His hooded gaze roved over her and she wasn't sure where the energy to blush came from, but she still felt the heat rise up her cheeks. Then he shoved his fingers through his hair and turned away, hitching his jeans back up over his lean hips.

She yanked her turtleneck down over her breasts. Her panties were a lost cause and she pulled on her jeans without them. Then she put on the discarded sweater and buttoned it up, right up to her neck.

Not that it did any good now.

She balled up the torn panties and ducked into the small powder room, then closed and locked the door as if she were in some danger of him busting in on her.

The woman who stared back at her from the mirror was wild-eyed and flushed.

She looked away. Then she used the toilet, washed her hands and splashed water over her face. She left her panties in the bottom of the small round waste basket next to the pedestal-style sink, and when she couldn't linger in there any longer without feeling like a coward, she left the room and followed the hallway into the kitchen.

He was standing by the open refrigerator drinking orange juice straight from the carton.

She looked away from the long sweep of his tanned back.

The broom was still propped against the wall where she'd left it the last time she'd been there and she went still.

Everything looked the same as it had the last time she'd been there two months ago, she realized.

From the swept-up pile of glass to the upended bookcase. Right down to the broken violin. Only he'd moved that to the middle of the table, where it sat like some sort of macabre centerpiece.

"Casey."

He didn't look at her. Just put the orange juice carton back and continued staring into the depths of the refrigerator, which even she could see contained very few items on its shelves. "You want something to drink?"

She looked at the violin again. "I want answers."

"No, you don't. Trust me."

Feeling shakier inside than ever, she moved around the island and set her hand on his back. She slowly pressed her mouth against the small scar on his shoulder blade. Felt him stiffen.

But he didn't move away.

And she took strength from that.

"If you expect me to believe that everything is fine, that *you* are fine, then you should have cleaned up this mess weeks ago."

"I didn't figure you'd ever be back to see it." He pushed the refrigerator door closed and looked down at her. A storm she couldn't understand—one he wouldn't explain—brewed in his gray eyes. "You were right when you said you didn't know who I am."

She swallowed. Wet her lips. "Are you going to tell me?"

His jaw canted. He looked as if he was going to answer and every fiber of her being felt on edge, waiting.

But then his expression smoothed out and "I'm going to bed" was all he said.

Her shoulders sank and she watched him start to walk out of the room. But after several steps, he stopped. "Do you want to come?" His voice was low. Raw.

Everything inside her tightened.

She nodded, even though he hadn't looked back at her, so had no way of seeing it. "Yes." The word sounded as strangled as it felt.

He looked over his shoulder at her then.

"Yes," she repeated. More clearly. More certainly.

His eyes narrowed, black lashes nearly obscuring the thin gleam of gray.

Then he turned and led the way.

Feeling more uncertain than she'd ever felt in her life, Jane followed him up the staircase. When he reached the top, he flipped on another light, illuminating the second-floor hallway and the open doors leading off it. Bedrooms, she could see as she passed them.

He went into the last one straight ahead at the end of the hall.

There was a raw spot on the inside of her cheek from the way she kept chewing at it and she made herself stop as she entered his bedroom. Despite the dim illumination from the hallway light, she could see the bed was king-size. Unmade.

Unlike the mess he'd left unattended downstairs, neither of these facts surprised her.

"Why do you want such a big house when it's just you?"

"I don't want to talk, Janie," he said wearily.

She swallowed down the words that kept rising nervously inside her.

He didn't bother taking off his clothes, just yanked

off his boots before throwing himself down on top of the mattress. "Do you need to take out your contacts or anything?"

Her palms felt sweaty. She swiped them down the seat of her jeans as she shook her head. "They're extended wear." Just because she didn't usually sleep with them in didn't mean she couldn't.

He bunched one of the pillows under his neck. Then he held out his arm. "Come here."

She felt like a virgin all over again.

Tugging nervously at the bottom of her sweater, she toed off her tennis shoes before sitting cautiously on the side of the bed.

"Relax," he muttered, tugging her unceremoniously down beside him. "I just want to sleep."

She made some sound that was unintelligible even to herself and turned onto her side. He dropped his arm over her waist, flattening his palm against her belly, and pulled her against him.

She exhaled slowly.

"Feels weird, doesn't it?"

She swallowed. "Yes."

"You want to leave?"

Her eyes burned again. "No," she whispered.

His chest rose and fell against her back as he sighed. "You'd be better off if you did."

She stared hard at the rectangle of light shining through his bedroom door from the hallway. "Why?"

He was silent so long she wasn't sure he'd answer. "Because I'm never gonna be able to be the man who fits your plan."

"Plans change," she whispered. Feelings changed. Hopes. Dreams. All were subject to change, able to turn on a dime simply because of one particular man.

Then he sighed again. "Not all plans," he said quietly.

The gold rectangle of light blurred around the edges. She blinked and a tear leaked out. "Sex is the easy part, isn't it?"

"It's everything else that's hard," he finished.

She sniffed.

"Are you crying?"

"No," she lied.

"Yeah. Me either," he murmured. Then he kissed the top of her head. "Go to sleep, Janie. Morning'll be here soon enough."

And it was.

The sun was shining through the unadorned windows right onto her face when Jane woke.

She knew immediately that she was alone in the bed. She stretched and turned onto her back, studying Casey's room in the fresh light of day.

He had a cluster of frames holding pictures of his sisters and their families on top of the old-fashioned dresser across from the bed. An untidy stack of thick books sat on the floor beneath the three windows that lined one wall. Next to them was a baseball bat, a pair of snow skis and a wicker hamper overflowing with wildly colored shirts and blue jeans.

Feeling stiff, she rolled off the bed, then spotted the alarm clock sitting on the nightstand. Horrified at the time, she bolted from the room, only to run back in, sliding a little in her socks, to stuff her feet into her tennis shoes. "Casey?" She called his name loudly as she thumped down the staircase, but there was no answer.

She hadn't really expected one.

The house felt empty.

She might have fallen asleep in his arms, but waking in them was obviously more than he was willing to allow.

And, honestly, it was probably more than she could handle.

She went into the kitchen, yanked open his refrigerator and took a few gulps straight from the very same orange juice container he'd drunk from hours earlier. She quickly replaced it and turned to go.

She had just enough time to drive home and change before she needed to open up Colbys again.

But her gaze landed on the broom. The broken glass.

It wasn't the mess that bothered her anywhere near as much as the mystery of what had caused it. Or why he'd left it to sit there for all this time.

She abandoned the plan to go home and instead found the dustpan in the cupboard where the broom had been and finished the job of sweeping up the debris. She muscled the tall wooden bookcase back into an upright position and inched it back and forth until it was situated flat against the wall. She couldn't do anything about their broken glass, but she arranged the picture frames back on one of the shelves anyway and stacked the books on another.

His choice of reading material was eclectic. Everything from World War I histories to the latest suspense bestsellers to essays on world politics, with a whole bunch of computer textbooks in between.

When she had everything picked up from the floor, she dusted her hands together and turned to go.

But the sight of the violin sitting on the table made her hesitate.

She carefully picked it up, holding it in both hands as she studied the broken neck. What she knew about violins would fit on the head of a pin. But maybe it could be fixed.

Maybe that was why he still had it.

But even as she considered that, she dismissed it. If Casey had wanted it fixed, it would already be done.

Instead, along with the upended bookcase, he'd kept it here like some sort of...reminder. Of what, she had no clue.

She turned the instrument over, studying the back of the warm-looking glossy wood. Hayley's grandmother was still staying with Hayley and had mentioned a familiarity with violins. If nothing else, maybe Vivian would have some advice. She scrounged around his drawers until she found a pen and wrote out a note on a paper towel. Then she tacked it to the front of the refrigerator with the bottle-opener magnet she'd found in the same messy drawer where she'd found the pen.

Having whittled away the limited time she had to drive home, she darted back up the stairs into the bathroom attached to his bedroom. She raced through a shower so fast the water never had a chance to get more than lukewarm and washed with soap that smelled like him. Then she ran his minty toothpaste around her teeth with the tip of her finger. She used his deodorant and dragged his short black comb through her hair, which she twisted into a braid that she fastened off with a yank of dental floss. She'd find something more suitable in her office desk once she got to Colbys.

Then, feeling as if she were committing some sort of crime, she opened his closet door in hopes of finding some sort of presentable shirt she could wear. The choices were thin, not surprising considering the quantity of empty hangers and the size of the pile of shirts overflowing his hamper. She took down a familiar red shirt with blindingly neon fish romping across the front and replaced her turtleneck shirt with it. She rolled up the too-long cuffs and tied the too-long hem around her waist. Then she poked through his dresser drawers until she found a clean pair of underwear.

The boxer briefs were pale gray and made her feel a little unsteady when she pulled them on. They were loose, but they were better than going commando to the pool tournament. And mercifully, they didn't show through her white jeans. She yanked on her sweater and went back downstairs. She retrieved the wounded violin and let herself out the front door.

His truck was gone from the driveway. At least it was proof that he hadn't been hiding somewhere inside the house, waiting for her to leave. Given that fact, it wasn't much of a stretch to guess he'd probably gone into Cee-Vid while she'd slept.

She set the violin on the seat beside her and drove the short distance to Colbys, where people were already congregating in front of the entrance to the grill and around the pool tables in the parking lot. She could smell bacon in the air and knew that her restaurant, at least, had gotten off to a timely start that morning.

Unlike its owner.

Swallowing her discomfort, she pinned a cheerful smile on her face as if it were just another day in the life and sailed past the small crowd at the door. She unlocked it and slipped inside the bar, scurrying around like a madwoman, flipping on lights as she went.

"You're late," Jerry said from the archway to the restaurant. "You're never late."

She barely gave him a glance. "Guess there's a first for everything. You set for the day? Need anything?"

He gave her an odd look. "Everything's running on schedule. 'Cept for you."

She ignored that and hustled past him into the storeroom, where she pulled off her sweater and grabbed a black apron to tie around her waist, the better to disguise the fact that she was wearing yesterday's jeans. Then she retrieved the register tills from the safe and headed back out front.

Jerry was still standing in the archway.

"Don't you have some cooking to do?" she asked pointedly.

He didn't budge. "You all right?"

Other than feeling stupidly weepy every time someone showed unexpected compassion?

She slid the first till into a register and pushed it closed. "I'm fine." When he still didn't move, she sighed and looked at him. "Jerry. I am fine. It was just kind of a crazy day yesterday."

He finally made a face. "I'll say. Never personally known any female who had two men literally fighting over her."

"Jerry—"

He held up his hands in surrender. "I'm going, I'm going. But you might want t' think about finding some different clothes unless you want everyone coming in here seeing your little walk o' shame."

She flushed and jammed the second till into place. So much for Casey's red shirt. "Go do what I'm paying you for," she grumbled, and was glad when he finally left the archway.

As soon as he was gone, she picked up the phone and called Hayley, asking her to bring her some clean clothes.

Thankfully, her very intelligent, learned counselor friend didn't question why she needed them.

She just brought them.

And when her eyebrows shot up upon seeing the garish oversize shirt that Jane was wearing, she didn't offer any comments except a toothy, delighted grin.

Chapter Thirteen

"You need to tell her."

Casey was sitting in his office while Axel closed the door to Control, where Casey could no longer enter. There was no point pretending he didn't know who his cousin meant. No point in pretending he didn't know what it was he needed to tell her.

Whether or not he'd been suspended from Hollins-Winword, he knew that Axel had just spent the past three hours running a lead into the ground on McGregor, who'd reportedly been spotted in Havana. It was the first sign in nearly two months that the agent might still be alive.

And Casey, through no one's fault but his own, had been barred from doing anything about it.

"We don't tell outsiders about Hollins-Winword," Casey retorted. His cousin, of all people, was on intimate terms with that inviolate rule. Axel had told Tara before they were married that he wasn't just the horse breeder most people thought he was only because her life had been in danger.

And now Ax was giving him an arid look. "Jane's not exactly an outsider. If she were, you'd have had a one-, two-, maybe three-night stand with her and moved on like you always used to after you got rid of that twit Caitlyn."

That "twit" had gotten rid of Casey the same way Jane would if she learned about his sterility.

"No." He pulled open his office door and they walked back into the open-plan area where Cee-Vid's legitimate gaming business was conducted. It was Saturday and the place was deserted.

They reached the front entrance of the building and went out into the cold morning sunshine that made a mockery of Casey's dark thoughts. The doors snicked closed behind them, automatically locking.

"Your life would be a lot easier if you'd just admit you are in love with her," Ax said as they headed for their trucks, parked side by side in the big parking lot.

"I'm not—" He bit off the denial and shook his head. His cousin was trying to get under his skin—something at which he'd always excelled. "You're letting those backflips you do every time Tara smiles at you mess with your head."

Ax laughed silently. "You'd be happy doing backflips for your woman, too, if you'd stop fighting it. I've been where you are, man. Suspension's a hard thing to swallow. You'll suck it up, same as the rest of us have had to do, resolve the problem and move on."

"And if it can't be resolved?"

Axel eyed him over the top of his truck. "We're going to find McGregor," he said. "We'll find him alive. Or we'll find him dead. Either way, we'll find him."

The mystery surrounding the missing field agent still plagued Casey. But he'd meant the situation with Janie.

"Unless he turned."

Axel's lips compressed. Casey knew his cousin didn't want to think McGregor had gone bad either. "We'll still find him," he said evenly. Then he deliberately lightened his tone. "It's the beginning of the holiday season. The whole family's gonna be together later for the tree lighting. Try to enjoy it. Might be good for you." Then he got in his truck and drove off. He was heading out to the place he shared with Tara and their two boys to pick them up and bring them back to town for the day's festivities.

Casey got in his own truck more slowly.

Waking up beside Jane—even clothed the way they'd been—wasn't like anything Casey'd ever experienced. And leaving her there, snoring softly with her hands tucked under her cheek like an innocent child, had been harder than he wanted to admit.

But if he hadn't left her there, hadn't sought sanctuary at Cee-Vid—even though that particular sanctuary was a shadow of what it should have been—staying until she'd wakened would have been even harder.

He might have slept soundly through what had been left of the night for the first time in months, but that didn't mean he was able to look in the mirror without seeing the reflection of a coward staring back at him.

And he hated a coward just as much as he hated a cheater.

He knew she'd be at Colbys by now. In the throng of her pool tournament contestants and more paying customers than she knew what to do with.

There was no reason he needed to show his face. Playing in the tournament was an excuse to be near her and he was tired of pretending otherwise.

Maybe he was just plain tired of pretending.

So he drove out of the parking lot and headed downtown.

There was even more of a crowd than there had been the day before. He was forced to park several blocks away, and even that spot wasn't entirely legal, if any of Max's minions decided to go write up parking tickets.

When he reached Colbys, he threaded through the crowd spilling over from the parking lot into the street. Colbys was an institution around Weaver. It had started out as just a bar long before he was born. Then somewhere along the line, the grill had been added. But never, not once, had it been as successful as Jane had made it.

He had no right to feel pride over that, but he did.

He managed to wedge himself through the doorway and spotted her right off. Wearing black jeans and a white sweater, perched on top of the ladder, updating the pool scores. While he'd been cooling his heels at Cee-Vid, the field had been whittled down to four contenders, including his own father.

For the first time that day, he felt an actual smile on his face.

Jane didn't notice him as she backed down the ladder and laughed at something someone said.

"You going to play human roadblock or move and let a person get inside?"

At the familiar, laughing voice, he pulled his attention away from Jane's smiling face and looked back to see his sister J.D. Her green eyes were sparkling. He dutifully moved aside and gave her a hug. "Where's the rest of the crew?"

"Kids are all out at the big house—" which was how she referred to the main house at the Double-C ranch "—and Jake'll be along soon. He dropped me off out front so he could find a parking place. Can you *believe* this turnout? Guess that's one thing good to come out of the snow being so late this year." Her hair was up in a ponytail, the same as Jane's was, but J.D.'s was nearly white-blond and short in comparison to the long, waving golden tail Janie sported.

His sister slid her arm companionably through Casey's. "Haven't seen you in a while. You haven't been to many Sunday dinners lately."

The family—whoever was available, including aunts, uncles, cousins and grandparents—always got together on Sunday afternoons for dinner. They rotated locations, but there was *always* some sort of weekly get-together.

In the past few months, he'd been absent even more than usual.

"Work's probably been keeping you pretty busy," his sister chattered on. "So you're bringing Jane this evening, right? Everyone'll be in town and present for duty at the tree lighting."

"We'll see."

She gave him the "I'm your big sister" look she'd been giving him all her life. "You're *bringing* your girlfriend, Casey."

"She's not—" He gave up. There was no word to accurately describe what Jane was, so why try? J.D. might not know about Hollins-Winword, but like most of his family, his sister had still decided she knew what was what. No amount of talking on his part would change her mind.

"Heard how you popped Arlo one," she continued blithely. "Nearly fell off my chair. Never even knew you had a temper lurking inside you." She poked him in the side, right where she knew he was ticklish. "Turns out my unflappable brother has a jealous streak. Who knew?"

He grabbed her finger before she could jab again. "Just

because I love you doesn't mean I won't break this thing off."

She grinned and patted his cheek. "I'm *so* afraid."

Then the door opened again behind them and her husband, Jake Forrest, entered. "Would've been easier to ride horses into town than find a parking place," he said in greeting. He stuck out his hand to Casey and clapped him on the shoulder as they shook hands. "Heard you're going for the Golden Gloves." Jake's lips twitched. "Never knew you were the boxing sort."

Casey grimaced. "Suppose it's too much to hope my own family would let me live that one down."

"Way too much," J.D. agreed. "I'm more likely to punch someone than you are."

Since everyone around had evidence to the contrary, Casey just shook his head. "When're Angeline and Brody getting here?"

"This afternoon. Angel was hoping Sofia and Early would get their naps in on the drive over. She's dreaming, if you ask me, because I also know they're bringing a couple of their new pups along for Uncle Matt to check out. He's wanting a new dog for the Double-C."

Casey nodded toward the wall. "D'you see the leaderboard up there?"

J.D. saw their father's name and let out a whoop. "You go, Daniel Clay!" She grabbed Jake's arm. "Come on. Let's go find him."

His brother-in-law gave Casey a wry smile and indulgently followed as J.D. dragged him into the crowded bar.

Jane had written in the starting times for the games next to the finalists' names. Even if he was pleased about his father's progress, Casey still wasn't particularly in the mood for socializing. And he definitely wasn't in the mood for explaining why. So rather than hang out in the crowded bar until his dad's game began, he worked his way around the perimeter and slipped through the storeroom door.

Janie's office door was closed but not locked and he went inside. He sat down on her squeaky desk chair and studied the brand-new computer sitting on top of the desk.

At least she'd gotten one.

He booted it up and saw immediately that her old files had been transferred over and when, and that she'd barely used it since.

He didn't have to work hard to imagine her sitting right where he was now, cursing the new computer with every keystroke.

Jane and computers barely mixed.

In only a matter of minutes, he'd reorganized the system so it would at least appear more like what she was used to. She was even linked to the internet at long last, though her security levels were pathetic. He reset everything, including her woefully predictable passwords so she'd have at least a modicum of security against the typical hack attempt. Then, since he was there with nothing better to do, he beefed up her firewall and virus software and made sure she was set for automatic backups.

She'd want to brain him for interfering, but the changes were done and she was too practical to insist they be undone.

Then, because his dad's game was still some time off, he leaned back in the chair, making it squeal even more wildly, propped his feet on the corner of her desk by the picture of her little sister and closed his eyes.

Which was exactly the position he was in when Jane, running into her office for a new black marker since the

old one was running out of ink, discovered him. Propri-
etarily snoozing in *her* office, his dusty boots propped
on *her* desk, while the words "Have you seen these fish?"
scrolled up and down and around on her computer screen
in a dizzying array of colors with animated neon-colored
fish swimming in the background.

She should have shoved his boots off the desk. Taken
him to task for messing with her computer, because he
obviously had. The shirt she'd borrowed from his closet
was folded on top of her file cabinet. It had clearly been
his inspiration for the screen saver.

Instead, she paused for a moment and studied his face.

"You come in here for a reason, or just to admire the
wares?"

She huffed, but only to maintain good form. "I should
have known you weren't asleep."

He didn't move an inch except to open one eye. "I was
until you started breathing all hot and heavy."

She couldn't quite keep her amusement under wraps,
but she unceremoniously took him by the boots and lifted
his feet off the desk anyway.

The chair positively squawked as it tilted far backward.

He shot out an arm to steady the chair, grabbing on
to the nearest object.

Which happened to be her leg.

She let go, and his boots hit the floor with a thud.

Unfortunately—or fortunately, depending on one's
viewpoint—he didn't let go of her.

Instead, his hand slid upward from the back of her
knee to flirt with the back of her thigh, his touch ridiculously warm through her denim jeans.

Her brain just sort of short-circuited. "I took your violin," she blurted.

His fingers paused their merry little tiptoe. His eyebrows lifted slightly.

"I, um, I thought I'd see if it could be fixed." She moistened her lips. "I know I had no business. I mean, it's *your* violin, but—"

"It's okay."

Her words dried up in her throat. "It is?"

He swiveled in the chair, sliding his other hand behind her other thigh.

"Yes. But why'd you care?"

She had a building full of people and all she could think about was the fact that, sitting as he was, his head was on a level with her breasts and his fingertips were roving over her rear.

"Because—" She broke off. Swallowed hard and tried not to tremble. "Because I think the violin matters to you and—" And he mattered to her. "And you, um, you obviously haven't had time to do anything about it," she managed with careful tact, when what she wanted to do was demand answers that she knew better than to expect.

His lips twisted. "It was my grandmother's," he said after a moment. "My dad's mom. Squire's first wife. Her name was Sarah."

She'd lived in town long enough to have heard the general history of the Clays. She knew that Squire Clay's first wife had died when his five sons were still young, so there was no way that Casey could have ever met the woman. "It must be pretty old."

He made a small grunt of agreement. "The old man didn't save much of hers when she died," he added after a moment. "Couldn't bear it, according to my dad."

"But he saved the violin," she murmured.

His wide shoulders rose and fell as he nodded. She'd heard him play just that one time. But she could only imagine how tiny the obviously cherished instrument must have looked in his big hands.

She slowly lifted her hand and tentatively brushed her fingers through his hair.

He sighed again, his head falling forward to rest against her stomach.

Her throat went tight. "How long have you had it?"

"Since I was in second grade." He sighed again, slid his hands upward and lightly slapped her butt, breaking the spell as he sat back once more. "Squire'll nail me to a tree."

Her hand fell to her side. "I think you're nailing yourself," she murmured, "with no help needed from your grandfather at all. Every single day when you saw it sitting there broken."

He didn't deny it. "You've got some pool games to get started."

She wanted to protest, feeling as if something important was just out of her grasp.

But he was right.

So she leaned over him to grab a fresh marker from one of the drawers in her desk and felt his hand slide over her back, light as a whisper. She straightened, and that light touch fell away almost as if it had never been. She stared into his silvery eyes. "Casey—"

"You like cheesecake?"

She blinked, thoroughly off balance. "I… What?"

"My grandma Gloria, she makes a hell of a cheesecake."

Gloria being Squire's wife. The woman he'd married, so the stories went, decades after losing his beloved Sarah.

"You shouldn't miss it," he went on. "She's bringing

it to the tree lighting. So, you know…maybe you should come with me. So you can have a piece."

Her heart squeezed. She could feel a smile tug at her lips. "Are you asking me out on a date, Casey?"

He grimaced, but the delight curling inside her had too strong a foothold to be denied. "I'm just saying if you want some cheesecake, I can make sure you get some. You don't know my family, sport. They're vultures when it comes to good food."

"Okay."

He waited a beat, almost as if her quick response had surprised him. But then he nodded once, sitting up a little straighter. "Okay." He rolled the chair back a few inches and stood abruptly. "Just, uh, head on over to the park when you're finished here." He edged past her through the doorway.

Again, she was afraid something was slipping through her fingers. "You're going to hang around for the rest of the tournament, aren't you?" she asked quickly.

He didn't look particularly enthusiastic, but he nodded. "Yeah. I'll be around."

"If I were a betting woman, I'd say your dad's got a lock on winning," she added, wanting more than anything to see a smile come back into his eyes.

The corner of his lips did tilt, but that was the extent of it. His silvery eyes were still solemn. Haunted. "Looking that way," he agreed. "He's even better at poker, though I'll deny it if you tell him I said so."

She smiled as he'd meant her to. "I've gotten away with holding a few pool tournaments. Don't think I could get poker in under the law's radar."

"That's why everyone plays their games in private." His gaze dropped to her lips and she felt warm, but a loud cheer from out in the bar centered her.

She tightened her fingers around the marker she'd all but forgotten and briskly pushed her hand against his shoulder so she could leave the office. "That noise out there proves there's no privacy around here today, so it's a good thing there are only billiards on the schedule."

He reached the storeroom door before her and gave her a look as he pulled it open for her. "Definitely a good thing," he murmured.

Feeling the warmth turn into a hot blush, she looked away and hurried past him out into the bar where the scoreboard was still waiting for her. Feeling as though every eye in the place must surely be watching her—and knowing how ridiculous a notion that was—she diligently tended to her business and tried not to be too distracted when Casey joined the knot of family members clustered at one side of the room.

And she tried not to wish, too hard, for the rest of the day to pass quickly so she could move on to the tree lighting already. To his grandmother's cheesecake.

To him.

Chapter Fourteen

The only thing missing was snow.

Jane stopped herself from running across the street into the park and instead approached at a calm pace, which, she realized, just gave her more time to admire the dozens of Christmas trees arranged around the pavilion. With the sun setting behind it, the place would have been the quintessential winter wonderland if not for the fact that the first snowfall of the season had yet to fall.

Not that the lack of snow meant it wasn't cold.

It was. And as she tugged the collar of her wool coat closer around her neck and tamped down the nervous excitement curling around inside her belly, her shaky breath sent vapor circles around her head.

A band was playing "Jingle Bell Rock" with more enthusiasm than skill as she made her way into the thick of people who'd already arrived. She could have gotten there earlier. She'd closed up Colbys a few hours after crown-

ing Daniel Clay the tournament winner, sending everyone home so they'd have a chance to attend the town's
celebration if they chose. But after closing, instead of
heading across to the park like Merilee and the others,
she'd gone home. Taken a proper shower. Worked some
order into her long hair and some cosmetics onto her face
and dabbed perfume onto her pulse points. She'd dressed
in her best black jeans and a red cashmere sweater. Buttoned the bright gold buttons running down the front of
her new black wool coat, which hugged her torso before
swirling out around her thighs.

Whether or not Casey considered it a date, everything
inside Jane *did*.

And now, clutching the disposable pan filled with
thick slices of Jerry's popular meat loaf against her mid-
riff, she was torn between turning tail and running away
like a coward or racing pell-mell forward until she found
Casey in the crowd.

In the end, she did neither. She carried the container
of meat loaf over to the buffet tables that were being
manned by volunteers from the tree-lighting committee. "Hope this isn't too late," she offered as she eyed
the dishes already there.

"Food's never too late," Pam Rasmussen assured her
brightly. Ordinarily, she was a dispatcher over at the sheriff's office, but tonight she was wearing her mantle as
chairperson of the committee. She took the pan and deftly
found a space for it between a platter of fried chicken
and three pots of steaming chili. "Heard you had a great
turnout for the tournament, despite the brouhaha between
Arlo and Casey."

"I did." She tried not to be too obvious looking for
Casey because Pam was one of the biggest gossips in

town, but Jane realized she was missing the mark when the other woman's grin widened.

"The Clays are all over there in front of the playground equipment," Pam said, pointing. "Right under one of the park lights. Think Casey's been waiting for you to eat," she added, and handed over two sturdy paper plates. "He's the only one of that whole crew who hasn't come through for some supper."

Jane didn't bother denying Pam's implications; she simply took the plates. "The park looks beautiful, Pam. Looks like half the town must have turned out tonight."

The other woman beamed. "The only thing we're missing is snow. We've always had snow before now."

Jane couldn't help but chuckle. "I was thinking the same thing just a few minutes ago."

"It won't matter once we turn on the tree lights," Pam continued, sighing happily. "It's my favorite time of year." She waved her hands. "Go on now and enjoy yourself."

"Thanks." Plates in hand, Jane turned from the tables and aimed in the direction Pam had indicated. She would have found the Clays despite the help; as usual, they were one of the largest groups there. And one of the rowdiest.

As she neared, she saw Casey's father standing in the center of them, holding up his tournament trophy in one hand while he held a little boy bundled in an orange parka propped on his other shoulder. It was plain for all to see which one he treasured more.

She couldn't help smiling at the sight and when Casey spotted her and came over, she nodded toward his dad. "If you ever decide you do want children, you won't have to worry about them lacking in love," she said lightly in greeting. "Guess you know that, though."

He seemed to sigh a little. "Yeah. I know that." He watched his dad for a moment as the man flipped the tot head over heels off his shoulder and set him on the ground to peals of the child's laughter. The boy immediately begged for more. "That's Early. Angel and Brody's boy. He's four," Casey explained.

She noticed then his other sister, dark-haired and somewhat exotic in comparison to J.D.'s heartland-and-wholesome blondness. Angel was watching her father and son with an indulgent expression. Despite the touchy topic of children where Casey was concerned, Jane couldn't seem to help herself. "Is his name really Early?"

"Nah. He's named Daniel, after my dad. But he was—"

"Early?"

"Not dangerously, like J.D.'s Tuck was. But Early already had the nickname."

"Well." Watching the boy was a treat. "He's darling. He looks like his mother."

The corners of Casey's lips kicked up slightly as he watched his nephew. "Yeah. He'll do."

Deciding to get away from the subject while the getting was good, Jane separated the paper plates and tapped him on the arm with the back of one. "A little bird told me you hadn't eaten yet." And she could see by the plates spread out over the three picnic tables taken up by Casey's extended family that if it was true, he was alone in that regard. "Not that I noticed a particular lack of food, but I brought a whole tray of Jerry's meat loaf, if you're interested."

He turned his gaze back to her and the intensity in his eyes sent all of her caution alarms ringing. Particularly when a curtain seemed to come down, and in a blink, he had his usual slightly wry expression. "Figured I'd be polite and wait," he said. "Didn't think I'd be waiting *this* long." He leaned down a few inches. "You smell like your own soap again instead of mine. All this effort for me, sport?"

She cursed her mushy knees and stiffened them, raising one eyebrow. "Never realized your sniffer was so finely tuned. But while you were obviously withering away during the, oh, forty-five minutes or so it took me to get here, I hope you managed to remember to save me some of your grandmother's cheesecake. That *is* what drew me here, after all."

His lips twitched and he cupped her elbow. His hands were bare. No concession to the cold temperature for him. And she could have sworn she could feel the heat of his touch through her wool coat.

She dismissed the silly notion. She was supposed to be a grown woman, not a teenager prone to such flights of fancy.

"Sure it wasn't my charming company?"

She gave him a look and his twitching lips stretched into a grin. His hold on her elbow tightened a little as he started walking. But instead of heading in the direction of the buffet tables, he steered her closer to the picnic tables crowded with his various family members. "Come say hello first."

Of course, she'd met all of them at one time or another. Was quite friendly with many of them. They frequented Colbys, and she'd served on a few volunteer committees more than once with several of his cousins. And until she'd hired Merilee and changed her own night off to Thursday to accommodate the other woman's schedule, Jane had taken weekly yoga classes with even more of them. But she still felt a jolt of nerves almost as if she were meeting them for the first time.

It was ridiculous. Annoying. Downright embarrassing,

actually. "I saw most of them a few hours ago when your father won the tournament," she reminded him.

"Yup. And you feel as stiff as a poker all of a sudden. Why is that?" His grin turned goading. "You're not nervous for some reason, are you?"

She tsked dismissively but because he was right, she moved forward even more quickly, taking the initiative herself as she aimed for his parents first, pinning a bright smile on her face as she plowed into the fray, greeting them as if her presence among the Clays were a perfectly ordinary thing.

But Daniel's mother, Maggie, ruined the whole thing by hopping to her feet and giving Jane an enthusiastic hug. "We're *so* glad you're joining us," she said as she squeezed. She was slender, about Jane's height, and her pale blond hair was nearly hidden by the cheerful red knit cap she wore. "I wasn't sure Casey would ever let the two of you out into the light."

Jane's face went hot and she stammered for a reply.

Maggie just laughed and squeezed her again playfully. "Don't be embarrassed, honey. We're just delighted you're here." Keeping her arm around Jane's shoulder, she pulled her along the tables, stopping every other step to share some comment with these people who were so familiar to Jane yet weren't.

She felt herself breaking out into a sweat beneath her coat from all of the attention she was getting. And Casey was no help at all. He'd stopped next to his dad, ostensibly to admire the tournament trophy. She figured he was really only saving himself from all this kindly meant torment and sent him a look that said so.

He just grinned and left her to his mother's clutches.

It was his grandfather Mr. Clay who finally offered some relief. Squire and his wife were sitting in fancy-looking folding lawn chairs rather than on the picnic-table benches, which seemed to be the only concession to their ages they were making. When Maggie presented Jane, he rose to his feet and snatched the paper plate that she'd pretty much mangled. He held it up to study.

"Good grief, child, you're not going to be able to hold any food on that, much less a piece of my wife's cheese-cake." His eyes were pale blue and they glinted with sharp humor as he tossed the ruined plate aside and com-mandeered her elbow from his daughter-in-law. Clutch-ing a walking stick in his other hand, he ambled with her toward the buffet tables. "Getting damn cold out here," he groused as they walked. "Don't s'pose you smuggled over some hooch from Colbys, did ya?"

She chuckled. Despite the walking stick, the gray-haired man stood almost as straight and tall as his sons and grandsons. And she knew from experience that he had a soft spot for a good Scotch whiskey. "Sorry." She tried not thinking about his first wife's violin still sitting in her truck. "Alcohol's not permitted in the park, even on a cold winter's night."

He grunted. "Seems the town council's getting mighty uptight these days 'bout that and every other little thing." He pounded the ground with the bottom of his walk-ing stick once for emphasis. "Half the adults here have prob'ly got a flask hidden in their pocket, spikin' their hot cocoa, which is what any smart person would do on a cold night like tonight. Got a good mind to get myself elected and whip those tight-asses into shape."

She grinned. Squire Clay was one of the backbones of Weaver. "Have you ever served on the council before?"

"Hell no," he said. "But I got a tad more time on my hands the older I get. Still think I could show them a thing or two."

"I can't think of anyone better," she assured him. The old man didn't mince words, play games or suffer fools. "You decide to run in the next election, I'll be the first one to offer a campaign contribution."

His laugh was almost silent, decidedly wicked and eerily like that of a particular grandson of his.

They'd reached the buffet table, where he handed her a fresh paper plate as if it were his wife's best china. "Now go fill it up, girl," he ordered. "Figure you need the fuel to keep up with Casey. That boy usually looks like he's moving slower 'n a snail when he's really running circles round us all."

"Stop bad-mouthing me, old man." Casey stopped next to them and dumped a ladle of overcooked green beans on her plate. "You're only doing it so you look better in Janie's eyes." His voice was tart but his fondness still rang through. "He's a flirt, sport, so stay on your toes."

Squire cackled. "Seems to me, you could've done a better job of flirtin' with this little filly. She wouldn't have needed to waste her time on Arlo if you hadn't been falling down on the job. His daddy was a milquetoast, and so's he." Squire slanted her a look. "No offense, honey. Arlo's a decent-enough fella, I s'pose, but I always figured you needed someone with more spirit."

"Decent," Casey snorted.

"I'm sure you never gave that any thought at all," Jane interrupted drily as she sidled out from between the two of them. "I'm hungry, so I'm going to leave you both to your debate." Before they could stop her, she hustled to the next table over. She grabbed a fried chicken leg and a slab of meat loaf, added a roll and a packet of butter and topped things off with a steaming cup of black coffee.

Pretending to ignore Casey, who'd quickly fallen in line behind her, she sipped the coffee and studied the turnout as if she were looking for an open seat, when the truth of the matter was that she felt too shy to head back to his family's tables on her own.

She spotted Sam, who was wearing her uniform under her coat, keeping an eye on the cluster of kids romping around the pavilion. There was no sign of Hayley and her grandmother, though Jane wasn't particularly surprised. When Hayley had brought Jane's change of clothes the morning before, she'd said her grandmother was reluctant to attend the outdoor celebration.

"Stop pretending you're not here with me," Casey said behind her, and nudged her toward his family's tables. "Everyone already knows otherwise."

"This just feels strange," she admitted.

"Being together? Out in the open?" His expression was deliberately wry. "I'm not the world's best catch, but you're damn hard on a man's ego, sport."

She made a face. Because he *was* the best catch. He always had been and she just hadn't wanted to admit it. "You were perfectly fine hiding in the shadows," she reminded him.

"You'd think, wouldn't you?"

Something in his tone gave her pause, but he was continuing forward and she either needed to keep up with him or get left behind.

She quickened her step.

They squeezed in between Angeline on one side and J.D. on the other. And before Jane could lift her plastic fork to her mouth, Casey warned his two sisters to behave.

"We always behave," J.D. said defensively, but her expression was positively unholy.

"I don't know what you mean," Angeline added, equally innocent.

"God save me from older sisters," Casey muttered.

Jane couldn't stop the laughter from escaping. "I *am* an older sister, too," she reminded.

Casey grinned and his gaze dropped to her lips. "Thankfully, not mine," he drawled.

Her mouth went dry and she barely managed not to squirm on the picnic bench.

J.D. waved her hand in the air comically. "Good grief. Anyone else feel that heat wave?"

"I did," Angeline said from the other side. "If that keeps up, the snow Uncle Matt predicted is going to melt into rain."

"Don't you both have rug rats you should be keeping an eye on? Would seem more important than reminding me what pains in the butt you were growing up."

J.D. laughed merrily and bumped her shoulder companionably against Jane's. "He must *really* like you," she said, not entirely under her breath. "I think we're actually getting under his skin. And that hasn't happened since he was fourteen and had a crush on Jenny Lee Sanders. Remember the way he mooned around over her, Angel?"

Casey sighed loudly and looked across the table to his sisters' husbands. "Guys, where's the help?"

"You're on your own, man," Brody said. He nodded toward Angeline. "She's the one I've gotta live with."

Angeline stood and rounded the end of the table. Her thick dark hair streamed down the back of her coat and her dark eyes sparkled with lively humor. "*Gotta* live with?"

Brody hooked his arm around her waist and pulled her off her feet onto his lap. "Gotta live with," he repeated, and gave her a smacking kiss.

"Get a room," J.D. suggested on a laugh.

Jane bit the inside of her lip, catching Casey's gaze

on her face. Beneath the table, she set her hand on his thigh. "Thanks."

He shrugged as if he didn't know what she meant, when it was plain to her that he did. "They're a crazy bunch," he said. "But I guess that's nothing you didn't already know."

Maybe. But this was the first time she'd been part of the "bunch" from the inside.

Then a noise from the pavilion drew their attention to Pam Rasmussen, who'd commandeered one of the band's microphones to thank everyone for coming and announce that the official tree lighting was about to commence. The drummer did a long drumroll and the entire crowd seemed to hold its breath in anticipation as they waited for the trees to light.

And waited.

And waited.

"Oh, for pity's sake," Pam finally said, sounding exasperated. "Somebody plug in the extension cord, will you?"

Laughter scattered around the park. Then suddenly the trees jumped to life, each one illuminated with hundreds of tiny white lights. The band started playing "Santa Claus Is Coming to Town" amid the applause and cheers that broke out. It didn't matter that the teenage boy singing lead had a voice that tended to crack every now and then, or that some of the trees hadn't lit at all.

It was still magical.

Looking around her, Jane saw the awestruck expression on young Early's face, echoed by a half-dozen others, and had to swallow the sudden knot in her throat.

"You're not looking at the trees," Casey said close to her ear, and she shivered a little.

"Look at Early," she whispered in return. "Have you ever seen a sweeter look on a child's face?"

Casey was silent for a moment. Then he exhaled, long and low. "There's something you need to know."

Still caught in the same web as Early and everyone else, she turned her head. Casey's face was only inches from hers and she lost the ability to breathe. "Hmm?"

He slowly nudged a lock of her hair behind her ear. Touched her chin with his fingertips, then shook his head a little. "Why are you here with me, Janie?" His low voice was barely audible.

He was straddling the picnic bench beside her; where her shoulder touched his chest, it felt wide and solid beneath his leather jacket. Her feet were cold inside her boots and her butt was almost numb from the wooden bench. But she felt surrounded by his warmth as the rest of the crowd seemed to disappear.

Her heart beat so loudly it was nearly all she could hear. And she couldn't keep the truth to herself anymore. "Because I'm in love with you," she whispered faintly.

He sighed again and slid his hand behind her hair, holding her head close to his. But his lips didn't touch hers. They grazed her cheek. "I'm sterile, Jane," he said so softly next to her ear that she wasn't sure she heard him right.

But when she went to pull back to look at his face, his hand turned to iron, not letting her move a centimeter. "I can't make a baby with you."

Her nose prickled and her eyes stung. "Casey—"

"Ever," he added. "It's not something that can be fixed or changed or treated. You want a baby and I'm not man enough for the job."

Then he let her go, pushed off the picnic bench and walked away.

It felt like an eternity that she sat there, frozen with shock.

But on the podium, the band was still claiming Santa Claus was on his way, the white lights on the dozens of trees were still twinkling and nobody around them—not even Casey's sisters—were paying them the least bit of attention.

He'd dropped a bomb on her world before walking away, and nobody had noticed.

She climbed off the picnic bench and hurried after him, not catching up to him until he was already out of the park and halfway down the block. And then she managed to overtake him only because she was running outright and he'd slowed, looking back at the sound of her boot heels.

"That's it," she called out breathlessly. They were alone on the street. The band was still audible but muted by distance. "You make your...your announcement and walk away?"

He turned, propping his hands on his lean hips. "Sorry if I didn't feel like hanging around to celebrate." His voice was tight.

She stopped a few feet away from him and sucked in a breath that was painful because the air was so darned cold. Obviously she needed to start running with Hayley and Sam, because she had a stitch in her side. "Why didn't you tell me?"

"I just did."

She exhaled. Took another step closer. "Casey—"

"It's not something I talk about," he said flatly. "With anyone."

"How do you know? That you're—"

"Shooting blanks?" His lips twisted. "I did a semester of college in Sweden and came down with the mumps while I was there. Turned out the vaccination I'd had as a kid wasn't real effective."

"You were engaged in college."

"Caitlyn. When I got back to the U.S. and told her, she dumped me flat." He shoved his hands in the side pockets of his jacket. "She wanted kids."

"If she'd really loved you, it wouldn't have mattered."

His hooded gaze drilled into her. "She was a self-centered twit who got into MIT on her daddy's money and her mama's family name. Marrying her would have been a disaster."

"But you loved her."

"I was twenty-one," he said. "And she was pretty as hell."

"And all these years later, you're still letting her rejection make you believe you're not *man enough*?" Her voice rose and she lifted her arms. "And you obviously must think I'm like her!"

He made an impatient sound. "I never said you were like her. You're not self-centered. You're not a twit. You're an intelligent, grown woman who knows what she wants. And what you *want* is what I can't provide!"

"*What I want is you*!" Her voice rang out, seeming to echo against the brick buildings on both sides of the street. He just stared at her with a grim, stoic look that made her want to launch herself at him. She hauled in another cold breath. "If I were the one with fertility issues, would you walk away because of it?"

"That's different."

She snorted. "How?"

"You're not a man."

"Thank God for that," she snapped. "Because one of us has to be able to think above her belt. Five minutes ago, I told you I was in love with you. Did that not register at all? Or does it just not matter? Am I really only your sex buddy after all?"

He yanked his hands from his pockets and took a step toward her. "Dammit, Jane, I'm trying to do what's right. You told me you wanted a baby. You wanted to get pregnant."

"Yes, I did. And I do. But not at your expense!" Her heart was in her throat but she stepped up to him until the toes of her boots nearly bumped his. "Tell me you don't have feelings for me," she demanded. "Tell me right now, to my face, that sex *is* all there is, and I'll do exactly what you seem to want." Her chest was so tight she felt dizzy. "I'll walk away. I'll sell Colbys. I'll go to Montana and bounce my sister's baby on my knee and start all over again where there's no chance of you and me bumping into each other every time we walk down Main."

"You're not gonna sell Colbys," he said.

"Try. Me," she said through her teeth, and knew down to her bones that the words weren't an empty threat. Weaver had become her home. But it would mean nothing in the end without him.

"And you're not leaving Weaver."

She stared him down.

He finally moved, pinching the bridge of his nose. The shaky strains of "O Holy Night" were coming from the park now. The sound of a car engine starting up in the distance was followed by a few more. It was dark. Cold. Now that the trees had been lit, it was no surprise the exodus had begun.

"There are lots of ways to make a family, Casey. You ought to know that better than anyone." Among his own extended family there had been foster children and adoptions and who knew what else. "If you don't want me, just admit it." Her eyes were tight with tears she wouldn't let fall. "But don't use your sperm count, or lack thereof, as an excuse. It's not sterility that'll make you less of a man to me. It's not being honest with me that'll do that."

"It's not just sex," he said flatly. "You know it's not just sex."

She exhaled slowly. Shakily. She knew him too well, though, to let relief fool her. "There's still a but in there, isn't there, Casey." It wasn't a question and the expression on his face gave her the answer.

She blinked hard and looked across the street at Colbys. The windows were dark, but the parking lot lights were shining down on the tent still set up there, and in the yellow gleam she could see a few snowflakes finally starting to fall. "You're more hung up on getting someone pregnant than I ever was on wanting to get pregnant," she said quietly. "Maybe that's your reason for throwing all of your devotion into Cee-Vid. I don't know. I just know that I love you, Casey. I have for a long while now. If you loved me, too—" she moistened her lips and sniffed hard "—if you trusted me, we could have figured out a solution together."

But he remained stoically silent. And it was obvious that no matter how hard she wished or how fervently she prayed for him to tell her that he did love her, trust her, it was not going to happen. And she took her cue from him.

She turned.

And walked away.

Chapter Fifteen

Hayley stared at Jane with shock. "*Sell* Colbys?"

It was Sunday afternoon and they were sitting inside her friend's living room. "I can't stay in Weaver, Hayley. Everything has to change or I'm going to be in exactly this same situation ten years from now. Loving a man who doesn't love me back."

"Casey didn't say he didn't love you."

"He didn't say anything." She'd told Hayley most everything that had happened the night before, but even with her closest friend, she wouldn't betray Casey's confidence about his sterility. She exhaled and picked up the box she'd carried in with her when she'd arrived. It contained his violin. "Do you think your grandmother would have some idea how to get this fixed?" She made a face. "Without anyone but us knowing about it?"

"You don't play the violin."

"It's Casey's."

Hayley absorbed that without comment. "I don't know," she finally said, and rose from the armchair where she'd been sitting. "Let me get her and we'll find out." She headed down the hall. "Grandmother? Can you come here for a minute?"

Vivian appeared, looking chicly turned out as usual in an expensive twinset and slacks. She was carrying two photograph albums. "Look, darling. I've finished the albums for your father and David." She patted the top of them with her slightly gnarled hand. "They hardly seem like good Christmas gifts," she said. "I could afford to give them—"

"The albums are perfect, Grandmother," Hayley interrupted. Jane could see they'd had the conversation more than once. "The fact that you kept all those old photographs will help show Daddy and Uncle David that you cared even when they thought you didn't." She took the albums and set them on a side table and gestured toward Jane. "We need your advice about a violin."

"Oh?" Looking pleased, the woman settled on the couch beside Jane and the box. Seeing the state of the violin, though, she frowned and set her reading glasses on her nose before carefully taking the instrument out of the box, tsking under her breath. "Who did such a thing?"

"It was an accident," Jane said quickly. "It belongs to a, uh, a—"

"Friend," Hayley supplied.

The word left a bitter taste in Jane's mouth. But she nodded.

Vivian turned it around to see the tiny markings on the back of it. "Do you know how valuable this is?"

"Probably not as much as it would be if it weren't broken," Jane murmured. "I know it's old, though. It belonged to my...to Casey's grandmother."

"Good Lord," Vivian said, sitting abruptly straighter as she studied the violin more closely. "Casey Clay," she said. "His grandmother was Sarah?"

"Mmm-hmm." It didn't seem odd that Vivian knew the detail. She'd been staying with Hayley for well over a month. "He hopes to repair it without upsetting anyone over the fact it was damaged."

"I imagine so," Vivian said. She sighed a little. "A person's sins coming to light is never easy."

Jane met Hayley's gaze at that. Her friend just subtly lifted her fingers as if to say *Who knows*? before focusing on her grandmother again. "So do you think it can be? Repaired, that is?"

"Oh, heavens, yes." Vivian's tone turned confident. "My father's shop is still in business." Her lips quirked. "Run, of course, by someone else since he's long gone. George is a distant cousin but he's kept the art in the business alive. We'll send it to him and he'll have it in perfect order again in a matter of days."

"That's it?"

Vivian stood and smiled at Jane. "That's it," she said. "Leave it here and I'll get it sent off tomorrow."

"That's very nice of you, Mrs. Templeton. Thank you."

"It's the least I can do after all these years," she said as she headed out of the room.

Jane looked at Hayley and raised her eyebrows. "What's that supposed to mean?" she asked under her breath.

"I have no idea," Hayley murmured. She moved the violin and box out of the way and sat next to Jane. "I'm not entirely sure she's not having some cognitive issues. She talks a lot about people and places of which, obviously, I have no knowledge. But then she'll say something like that and I don't know what to make of it."

"Have you just asked her?"

"Oh, yeah." Hayley nodded. "And she usually tells me how little she appreciates it. She told me the other day that just because she's old doesn't mean she's lost her marbles. She may be living with me and we're starting to get to know each other, but she's often *very* cryptic."

"Has she seen your dad and uncle yet?"

She shook her head. "They're still standing firm, refusing to see her. I've invited everyone over for Christmas Eve, though, and my mother promises me that she'll get Daddy here one way or the other." Her lips twitched with a hint of humor. "Nothing like family drama. Just wish it weren't my family."

"Guess that's one reason not to have a family at all," Jane said blackly.

Hayley made a sympathetic sound. "You really don't feel like you want to stay in Weaver after what's happened with Casey? I don't want to lose one of my two best friends."

"Would *you* want to stay?"

Hayley sighed. "As a therapist, I should say that every situation can be dealt with. But as your friend? I've never been in love before. Not really. So who am I to talk?"

Jane brushed her hands down the front of her jeans and stood. "Love is overrated anyway."

"You don't mean that."

She sighed and reached for her coat, which was draped over the arm of the couch. "No. I don't." No more than she'd meant it when she'd told Casey that passion was overrated. "But it would sure hurt a lot less if I did."

"You heading over to Colbys?"

"Gotta keep it in business if I'm going to put a for-sale sign on it."

Hayley made a face and hugged her. "Just promise not to do anything rash."

"I blew that opportunity three months ago when I told Casey I wanted to have a baby."

"And despite everything, you still want to get the violin fixed for him."

"Evidently, I can't do anything else for him," she said, and headed out the door.

The snow that had begun falling the night before had continued nonstop.

Hayley's front yard was covered in several inches of fluffy white, as were the streets and every other surface. Even the tracks left by Jane's truck tires in Hayley's driveway had nearly filled again during the time she'd been there.

She backed out and headed toward downtown, slowing to a crawl when she reached the corner of Casey's street. It would be so easy to turn. But why?

She wouldn't accomplish anything in driving by his house except cause herself more pain.

She passed the corner and kept going, telling herself it was good practice for the future.

Maybe one day she'd even manage it without tears running down her face.

"I walked away from your mother once," Casey's father said. He was standing in the front hallway of Casey's house, eyeing the duffel bag lying on the floor. "Hardest thing I ever did."

"She was also married to someone else at the time." Casey knew the story of his mother and her first husband, who'd been the Double-C ranch's foreman at one time before he'd embezzled a small fortune and run out on all of them, including Maggie and a newborn J.D. "Not the same thing."

"Not the same reason," his dad corrected him, "but walking away is walking away. And it took us too many years in between to get back where we both belonged. Here. Together."

"If I don't leave Weaver, Jane will."

"Yeah. That sounds familiar, too." Daniel scrubbed his hand down his face. "Look, son. I don't know the situation between you and Tris that's got you both wound so tight. Once I got out of Hollins-Winword, I was out for good and had no desire to look back. But I do know that the agency, for all the good it sometimes accomplishes, isn't a replacement for the things that matter. I've seen you and Jane together. Now that you've finally stopped this bull crap about hiding your relationship, I know how you feel about her. Stay and fight to make things work!"

Casey jammed a coat on top of the rest of the things he'd tossed inside the duffel. "And in a year or two years or even three, when she can't hide her disappointment anymore about having babies, what do I do then?"

"You face it together. That's what marriage is, Case. It's sticking together. Good days. Bad days. Hell, even the occasional indifferent one. You stick. You remember what the commitment was and you remember what drew you together in the first place. Because it doesn't go away. It just grows and gets deeper if you let it, until you can't imagine a life without that person being by your side."

"You never had to deal with being infertile," Casey said flatly.

"Seems to me you haven't been dealing with it either," his father fired back. "You learned about all this more than ten years ago and the first *we* hear about it is this afternoon during Sunday dinner at J.D.'s place when you finally saw fit to mention it!"

"I should have just left and kept it to myself," Casey muttered. But he hadn't, and his dad had been hot on his trail, trying to stop him.

"And leave your mother's heart broken." Daniel slapped the brim of his cowboy hat against his thigh, looking furious. "Of all of our children, you were always the one who felt someone else's pain the most. Even more than the girls. And this is what you're going to become? A man who runs away from the one he wants most?" He shoved his boot against the duffel. "You're a better man than that, Casey."

His father's censure was almost welcome. At least the abrasiveness of it wore down the edges of everything else that felt jagged and sharp inside him. He yanked the zipper closed on the bag, grabbed the straps and stood. "Obviously not." He started for the door but his cell phone rang before he got there.

He almost didn't look. But old habits died too hard and he was glancing at the display before he knew it. It was Seth Banyon, who was sitting in for Casey at Hollins-Winword during his suspension. Only the fact that it was Seth and not another member of the Clay family had him answering it. "Yeah."

"We found him." Seth's voice was terse. "McGregor. Sitting in a jail cell in some Podunk down in rural Mississippi. Using one of his known aliases. That's what popped for us. Tristan's on his way down there."

"He give you the okay to call me?"

"No. I figure asking forgiveness afterward is easier than getting permission beforehand." Seth rattled off a series of numbers and letters that Casey knew was the first-level access code to Control, which had been changed the second he'd been suspended. "Got that? I'm not repeating it."

"I got it." He ended the call and slid the phone into his pocket. He just wasn't sure what he wanted to do about it. Confirmation that McGregor was alive was only the tip of the iceberg where the agent was concerned. They still didn't know if, how or why he'd been involved in his partners' deaths.

He looked at his dad. "She also doesn't know what I really do at Cee-Vid. She doesn't know about Hollins-Winword. She'll think it's one more thing I've kept from her."

"And she'll be right," Daniel agreed, pulling open the door and walking out onto the porch. "You've got a hell of a mess on your hands, son. Stick around and clean it up. It'll be worth the effort if you do." He jammed his hat back on his head. "And if you don't, I'm afraid it's going to haunt you for the rest of your days. But whatever you do, you keep in touch with your mama. I'm not too old I won't come and find you and skin you myself if you don't. She's all torn up thinking how you'd been sick off in college all those years ago and never knowing about it. You're not going to make it worse. You got me?"

Feeling about as low as a snake and knowing his dad was more than capable of following up on his threat, Casey nodded. "I got you."

His dad's gray gaze pierced him. Then his tight expression finally eased. A little. He nodded once, turned on his boot heel and stomped down the steps, leaving footprints in the snow as he crossed to his truck.

Casey waited until his dad had driven away before finally moving. He locked and closed his front door and tossed the duffel in the passenger seat of his truck and started up the engine. He was glad McGregor was alive. But he couldn't think past Jane.

He didn't know where he was heading when he pulled out onto the street. He just drove.

And when he finally ended up in the circular gravel drive fronting the massive "big house" where Squire had raised Casey's dad and uncles, he exhaled, got out of the truck, walked around to the back of the house and went in through the mudroom.

Squire and Gloria now shared the big house with Matthew, who ran the cattle operation, and his wife, Jaimie. But Casey's grandparents were alone at the round oak table in the kitchen when he entered. Squire was drinking coffee, eschewing as he almost always did, the use of the cup itself, instead drinking from the edge of a nearly flat saucer balanced on his fingertips. Gloria was working the Sunday crossword from the newspaper. And neither one of them looked overly surprised to see him, despite the fact that they'd both been at J.D.'s place when he'd told 'em all he was leaving town.

Squire just shoved out a chair with his boot in silent invitation.

Casey didn't feel like sitting.

"I broke the violin," he said without preamble.

Cleanup had to start somewhere.

Gloria slowly raised her head, her graying auburn hair catching the light. He felt her gaze shift from him to Squire, then back again. Then she rose. "I think I'll leave you two to talk," she said. When she passed him, she patted Casey's cheek as if he were two instead of thirty-two.

The silence in the kitchen after she left was thick.

"It wasn't intentional," Casey finally added. "Well, it was, but not because I wanted to break it."

Squire sipped the rest of the coffee out of the saucer.

He'd drunk it that way ever since Casey could remember, claiming it cooled faster than in a mug; as anxious as he was to get caffeine into his blood, he wasn't anxious to burn the hell outta the inside of his mouth. When the saucer was empty, his grandfather set it down and leaned back in his chair, folding his arms across his chest. "You're gonna give me a crick in my neck if I gotta keep looking up at you, boy."

Casey still had no desire to sit, but he did. "It happened a few months ago. I should have told you before."

Squire pursed his lips but said nothing, which had the back of Casey's neck prickling. Because his grandfather had never been one to mince words.

"I'm sorry," Casey added doggedly. "Disown me. Curse me. Do whatever, because I know I deserve it."

"Clays don't disown," Squire said. "It was the other side, Sarah's family, who liked to do that sort of thing. Her mama was disowned for having Sarah out of wedlock and they never wanted to make up for it even when they had the chance." He curled his fingers and knocked his knuckles softly against the table. "You had that instrument since you were a pup. You think I didn't know it might get banged up a time or two?"

"It's worse than banged up. You're supposed to be tearing me into strips by now."

"Thirty, forty years ago, I would've. Sentimental value or not, it's just a *thing*, Casey. Sarah certainly understood that when she was alive. And now that I'm old as Methuselah, I understand it, too. If it can be fixed, fix it. Pass it on to the next generation someday. If it can't, then it can't."

"When did you start getting mellow, old man?" Casey's uncle Matthew had come in through the mudroom and had obviously overheard. He was holding a squirming Labrador pup in his arms.

"I've always been mellow," Squire countered.

Matthew made a face. "My foot," he muttered, and finally let the pup down to the floor.

The ball of yellow fur immediately scrambled under the table, brushing past Casey's legs. He reached down to pet the animal, but the puppy yelped and ran the other direction, toenails slipping and sliding on the wood-planked floor as he careened into the base of a cabinet before tearing off on yet another path.

"One of the ones Angel brought up," Matthew said with a shake of his head. "Dog'll never be a cattle dog. Can tell that already. He's afraid of his own shadow."

"He's a pup." Casey rose and managed to corral the little furball into a corner, where he hunched down on his butt and whined. Casey slid his hand beneath the puppy's round belly and picked him up.

"And a pretty one," his uncle agreed, looking amused. "But I need a dog who'll help work cattle, not another pet. Fortunately, the female your sister brought me reacted better in the barn. You like that little guy, you take him."

Casey immediately shook his head and started to hold out the dog. "I don't need a dog." The damned thing started licking Casey's hand. And peed on the floor.

"Think of someone who does," Matt suggested, tossing him a roll of paper towels. "Brody's already laid down the law to your sister that they're not taking any puppies back home with them. They've still got four more to give away."

Squire suddenly got up to pour more coffee into his saucer. "Take the dog, boy," he advised. "Consider it penance if you have to."

"A puppy for a broken violin?"

"Sarah liked a good Labrador," Squire said mildly. "And after all that bull-hockey you were yammering about this afternoon over at J.D.'s, seems to me having a dog might be a reason for you to give up your whole running-away notion."

Casey finished wiping up the small puddle and threw away the towels. The dog had moved on from licking Casey's hand to his arm, right through his long-sleeved T-shirt. "I'm not running away."

His uncle's eyebrows rose a little but he remained tellingly silent.

Squire, on the other hand, snorted loudly. "The only reason Sarah ever gave me the time of day in the first place was because she liked the dog I had back then." With his saucer balanced on his fingertips, he returned to his seat at the table without so much as a drip. He looked Casey square in the eyes. "Take the dog," he ordered flatly.

Casey took the dog.

He drove home and cleaned up another puddle of pee from his truck's leather seat and, once it was clean, covered it with an oversize folded towel to keep from having to do it again.

All the while, the dog followed on Casey's heels, though he didn't much seem to like the feel of the snow beneath his paws. "You're gonna have to get used to that, buddy," Casey told him, and lifted him up onto the towel-protected seat. "Around here, that stuff is usually on the ground for half the year."

The puppy propped his front paws on the console between the seats and stared expectantly at Casey with bright button-black eyes.

"You're crazy," Casey told the puppy. "She's not going to forgive me. There are too many things to forgive."

The puppy whined. Scratched his paw over the console.

He pinched the bridge of his nose. He really did need therapy if he was taking his cues from a *dog*.

But he found himself rounding the truck. Getting behind the wheel. "Don't you pee again," he warned, nudging the puppy back onto the towel. "Stay."

His little tail, small and stubby in comparison to his round body, wagged furiously and he let out a shrill, excited yip that had his entire body bouncing.

Casey made it to Colbys in a matter of minutes. The tent in the parking lot was gone and the Christmas trees had been pushed out to the sidewalk, lining the entire front of her building. He parked in the lot next to Jane's truck and zipped the puppy inside his jacket before going in through the grill door. Fortunately, all of the tables were filled with customers and he didn't get a second look as he strode through to the bar. Only Merilee was behind the taps, though, and when she spotted him, she jerked her head toward the storeroom door. "Back there."

One small mercy, he figured. At least he wouldn't have an audience.

He went through the door and not for the first time wished the thing had a lock on the inside. He passed the cooler full of kegs and stopped in the opened doorway of Jane's office.

She was sitting at the desk glaring at the computer and without wasting a beat, quickly transferred that glare to him. "You changed my password," she accused. "Yesterday while you were messing around with *my* computer, you changed *my* password."

He felt as if a year had passed since the previous morning. He picked up the picture frame holding the photograph of her sister's family and showed her the narrow piece of masking tape he'd stuck there on which he'd written down the password. "You should memorize it."

She peeled off the tape. "CclovesJC695," she read off slowly. She was silent for a long, long moment that had Casey's nerves burning. "You put this here yesterday morning," she finally said.

"Yeah."

Her throat worked. She didn't look at him. "What's 695?" Her voice sounded strangled.

"Best passwords have random numbers and characters. I figured you could remember six ninety-five, though. That's what you charge for a beer."

"You let me walk away last night without a word," she finally said. She pressed the tape flat on the desk in front of her. "You'd already left this for me, but last night?" She pushed to her feet and stared at him with wounded eyes. "Not. One. Word."

Inside his coat, the puppy squirmed silently, and he hoped to hell the dog wasn't peeing there, too. "Last night you weren't only talking about love. You were talking about honesty. And I haven't been."

She angled her chin upward, looking haughty even though he knew it was an act.

He managed to wedge himself inside her office and close the door behind him, putting another layer of privacy between them and her patrons. She raised an eyebrow but bumped into her chair noisily when she backed up, obviously anxious to put space between them.

The puppy whined a little and Jane's eyes narrowed. "What was that?"

He tried pretending ignorance. "What was what?"

She crossed her arms, her expression turning sharp. "Casey—"

He exhaled and unzipped his jacket, pulling out the

puppy, who was all too happy to escape, wriggling right out of his hands and onto the desktop, where he promptly knocked Jane's photograph off onto the floor. When he started to squat next to the keyboard, Casey hastily picked him up and moved him to the floor. It, at least, was tiled and could be cleaned easily.

Jane had plopped down onto her chair and was staring at both the puppy and Casey as if they'd turned pink and sprouted tutus. "That is a dog." She pointed out the obvious. "You brought a dog into my place of business."

"I wasn't gonna leave him in the truck. It's too cold outside."

She eyed him. "Casey—"

Even though there was barely room with the door closed the way it was, he crouched down in front of her chair and closed his hands over the arms so she couldn't swivel away from him. "My work at Cee-Vid is just a cover for what I really do," he said quietly. "For what several of us really do." The puppy was sniffing his way around the tight perimeter of the office, worming his way beneath the bottom of the metal desk drawers and popping out on the other side.

"A cover," she repeated, looking from the dog back to his face. "For what?" Her voice was tart. "Puppy breeding?"

"Spying."

Her lips twitched as if he'd just told a bad joke. "Yeah, right."

"Jane."

Her gaze flickered. She moistened her lips. "You're serious."

"Those two guys who died, remember?" He didn't need her nod to know that she did. "They were field agents working under my watch. It was my job to keep them safe and I didn't."

"Spies," she repeated faintly. "Like…spies. James Bond spies."

"A whole lot less glamorous," he corrected her, not entirely sure why he found that amusing but realizing that he did. "Hollins-Winword is a private agency that sometimes works with the government and sometimes doesn't. Sometimes it's as simple as keeping some rich guy's kids safe and sometimes it's an op that's years in the planning."

"Legally, though," she prompted, looking a little dazed. "Right?"

He hesitated. "Do you want me to whitewash it, Janie? Mostly, yes. But not always. Not entirely. And that's not going to change. Hollins-Winword is about doing what's right. And that sometimes gets into a gray area."

Her jaw loosened. "And this is happening in *Weaver*. Right under our noses. Why hasn't anyone ever found out?"

"Because we're very good at keeping secrets. And you'll have to keep it secret now, too."

"Then why tell me at all? Maybe I'll go blabbing it all over town!"

"Because you think I don't trust you, and I want you to understand just how much I do."

Her mouth slowly closed. She suddenly blinked and looked away, scooping up the dog to hold him in her lap. The puppy immediately pawed her breasts and tried to lick her chin. "What's his name?"

Baring Hollins-Winword's secrets was easier than baring his soul. "I was thinking we could pick out a name together," he said gruffly.

Her eyes lifted to meet his. "Why?"

"He sort of got pawned off on me," he admitted. Because it was a certainty that sooner or later she'd find out how he'd come to have the dog. "But he needs a family." His chest went tight. "And seems like you and I could start off with him."

She pressed her cheek to the dog's head but never took her eyes from Casey's. They'd turned wet and shiny.

"While we figure out everything else," he finished huskily. "If you're…willing."

She was silent for a moment. "He's quite the Christmas gift," she said slowly. "I don't have room for a dog in my condo. Look at the size of his paws already. He's going to be big as a moose."

"I have room for Moose, even if he is one. I have room for you. And he's not a gift. He's a promise." His jaw felt tight. "But I don't want to be someone you're settling for, Janie. You deserve everything you want. So when you change your mind down the line—"

She pressed her fingers over his mouth. "I'm not going to change my mind. We can have this discussion in a year. In five years. In fifty. I am not changing my mind. So we'll just become Weaver's newer version of Dori and Howard, two old geezers living together."

He pulled her hand away, holding it firmly in his. He knew where she was heading, and all his reasons for resisting kept slipping out of his grasp. "I'm not suggesting you live with me," he corrected her.

Her eyes were still wet, but a faint smile suddenly flirted with her lips. "So now you don't have room for me?"

"You said you wanted a husband." He leaned over the dog until his lips hovered next to hers. "Turns out I want a wife."

Her hands slowly rose and came around his shoulders.

"I don't know, Casey." Her words whispered against his lips. "We've only been out on *one* date."

"Is this what life is going to be like with you, sport?"

She nodded and her lips slid, light as breath, against his. "Probably. Why do you call me sport?"

He closed his hand behind her head, tilting it slightly. "Because you're my favorite thing to play with."

She sank her hand in his hair and pulled hard. "I'm not a toy."

"No, you're not," he agreed. He pulled back enough to look in her eyes. "You're the love of my life. So tell me you'll marry me and then shut up and kiss me."

She smiled slowly, her eyes glistening. "You're the love of *my* life," she returned. "And I will marry you."

Then she leaned forward to kiss him, but the puppy got in their way, slathering his tongue over their chins.

Laughing, tears still in her eyes, Jane pulled back only long enough to set the puppy on the floor. "Lie down, Moose," she said firmly.

And damned if the little pup didn't wag his stubby tail, turn in a circle and lie down with a contented huff.

Then she looked back at Casey. "Now. Where were we?"

He pulled her close, feeling the beat of her heart against his and finally accepting the truth that he'd take any chance as long as it meant she'd be his. "Here," he whispered, covering her mouth with his. "Always and forever, here."

* * * * *

MILLS & BOON®

Want to get more from Mills & Boon?

Here's what's available to you if you join the exclusive **Mills & Boon eBook Club** today:

- ◆ *Convenience – choose your books each month*
- ◆ *Exclusive – receive your books a month before anywhere else*
- ◆ *Flexibility – change your subscription at any time*
- ◆ *Variety – gain access to eBook-only series*
- ◆ *Value – subscriptions from just £1.99 a month*

So visit **www.millsandboon.co.uk/esubs** today to be a part of this exclusive eBook Club!